Bolan shook his head

He'd seen plenty of fanatics willing to die for their cause. Call it a gut instinct, but these two women didn't seem to be the type to take their lives for an abstract slogan. In Bolan's experience, this type of brutal self-sacrifice was committed for a dynamic personality.

This force, this entity, this malevolent being stood at the center of the maelstrom of violence threatening to storm across Germany.

Just who could inspire this kind of bloodshed?

D0932174

MACK BOLAN ®
The Executioner

The Don Pendleton's
Executioner ®

SILENT THREAT

A GOLD EAGLE BOOK FROM
W❂RLDWIDE ®

TORONTO • NEW YORK • LONDON
AMSTERDAM • PARIS • SYDNEY • HAMBURG
STOCKHOLM • ATHENS • TOKYO • MILAN
MADRID • WARSAW • BUDAPEST • AUCKLAND

Recycling programs
for this product may
not exist in your area.

First edition July 2010

ISBN-13: 978-0-373-64380-6

Special thanks and acknowledgment to
Phil Elmore for his contribution to this work.

SILENT THREAT

Printed in U.S.A.

The less reasonable a cult is, the more men seek to establish it by force.

—Jean-Jacques Rousseau
1712–1778

The true fanatic can be mesmerized by a charismatic leader, forced to harm or to kill in the name of the cause. My cause is Justice, and I'll mete out my brand of judgment to those killers with extreme prejudice.

—Mack Bolan

THE
MACK BOLAN
LEGEND

Nothing less than a war could have fashioned the destiny of the man called Mack Bolan. Bolan earned the Executioner title in the jungle hell of Vietnam.

But this soldier also wore another name—Sergeant Mercy. He was so tagged because of the compassion he showed to wounded comrades-in-arms and Vietnamese civilians.

Mack Bolan's second tour of duty ended prematurely when he was given emergency leave to return home and bury his family, victims of the Mob. Then he declared a one-man war against the Mafia.

He confronted the Families head-on from coast to coast, and soon a hope of victory began to appear. But Bolan had broken society's every rule. That same society started gunning for this elusive warrior—to no avail.

So Bolan was offered amnesty to work within the system against terrorism. This time, as an employee of Uncle Sam, Bolan became Colonel John Phoenix. With a command center at Stony Man Farm in Virginia, he and his new allies—Able Team and Phoenix Force—waged relentless war on a new adversary: the KGB.

But when his one true love, April Rose, died at the hands of the Soviet terror machine, Bolan severed all ties with Establishment authority.

Now, after a lengthy lone-wolf struggle and much soul-searching, the Executioner has agreed to enter an "arm's-length" alliance with his government once more, reserving the right to pursue personal missions in his Everlasting War.

1

The wet streets of Berlin reflected the headlights of passing cars and the multicolored glow of countless shop signs. The clouds covering the leaden skies appeared to give no ground to the approaching twilight, but as the rain grew colder, the coming darkness closed over the busy streets like a clenching fist. Heedless of the rain, dressed in a brown trench coat and matching snap-brim hat, a man crossed the street in front of a popular coffee shop. He was one figure among many, but his presence caught the eye of one of the shop's customers, who had taken a table near one corner. The table offered a good view of the large picture windows in front.

The man in the trench coat paused to remove his hat and run his fingers through his hair. His coat was open, and the watcher sitting in the corner noted the butt of the revolver just barely visible in the newcomer's waistband.

"You are not difficult to spot," said the man in the trench coat, moving to sit at the corner table without invitation.

"You're fairly conspicuous yourself," said Mack Bolan, aka the Executioner. "What's with the third-rate spy novel getup?"

The man in the trench coat knew Mack Bolan as Matt Cooper, and for all his faults was probably well aware that the name was an alias. "I don't see any reason to be insulted, Cooper," he said.

Bolan gave him a hard look. "You don't have something more important on your mind, Rieck?"

Adam Rieck, Bolan's Interpol liaison, grimaced. "A fair point," he said. He produced a folded sheaf of papers from inside his coat. "This is it."

Bolan took the papers, glanced around and began shuffling through them under the edge of the table. There were laser-printed color photographs, a complete itinerary and some computer-generated maps indicating where the itinerary stops correlated physically. Bolan nodded.

"This will be plenty," he said.

"Then I guess we'd better get going." Rieck nodded in turn.

Bolan eyed him again. "Taking you along wasn't part of the deal." Of course, he'd known that it very well could be, and Hal Brognola, director of the Sensitive Operations Group, whose base of operations was at Stony Man Farm, Virginia, had said as much in describing the operation.

"Germany is in trouble," the big Fed had said, speaking to Bolan from Washington using a secure, scrambled satellite phone.

"The whole country?" Bolan had asked.

"On certain levels," Brognola said. "You're aware of the push for greater security, greater governing controls on strategic industries worldwide."

"Sure," Bolan replied.

"The German government recently initiated a series of protocols intended to protect strategic industries from being bought out by what they call 'locusts'—potentially hostile foreign investors, 'undesirable' hedge funds, and so on. In today's political and war-fighting landscape, this is no surprise. Aaron and his team regularly monitor this type of activity."

"I follow you," Bolan said, knowing that Brognola referred to Aaron "the Bear" Kurtzman, head of the Farm's team of computer wizards.

"While following up on the proposed controls and investigating some of the investment funds flagged as 'undesirable' foreign interests, Bear and his people found a subtle pattern. They tracked it and produced a very disturbing picture, something that only becomes apparent when you look at investments in strategic industries a few steps removed. Holding companies controlling holding companies influencing local German investors, in other words, but ultimately all linked to a central source."

"Someone is buying into strategic industries in Germany. Someone with less than patriotic intentions."

"Yes," Brognola confirmed. "Specifically, a business entity calling itself Sicherheit Vereinigung, the Security Consortium. On its face, there's no reason a company wouldn't try to consolidate domestic industries when permitted, to secure a vertical hold on the market. But when that company does so but tries to conceal what it's doing, it begs the question… why?"

"The Security Consortium. Sounds bland."

"It's meant to," Brognola said. "They even have a Web site, Bear tells me. It's completely harmless at first and second glance—just another among a seemingly endless list of financial services and investment companies. This one is headquartered in Germany, but Bear and his people have uncovered several backdoor ties to international interests. Those including rogue nations like Syria and Iran, countries that definitely do not have the interests of the Western industrialized world at heart."

"There has to be more."

"There is," Brognola said. "Purchases of major German interests have gone mysteriously well for the Consortium. You might say they have miraculous corporate luck. If a local politician or businessman stands in the way of an acquisition, he either changes his mind quickly or has a perfectly explainable accident. No less than a dozen deaths, all officially classed as natural causes or freak misadventures, have been linked to chains of events that all ended in successful acquisitions by the Consortium."

"So you think they're muscling their way in, quietly."

"And insidiously," Brognola said. "More problematically, we theorize they have access to a potentially huge pool of foot soldiers, a dangerous group of people who are unpredictable. It's a group called Eisen-Donner, or 'Iron Thunder.'"

"Never heard of it," Bolan admitted. "Is it a gang?"

"It's a German cult, actually," Brognola said, "and an underground one. The government is less tolerant than some others when it comes to these modern religious groups. You recall the uproar over there regarding that Hollywood actor and his religious ties, the one who wanted to film the World War II movie on site there."

"Vaguely," Bolan said wryly. "I don't have a lot of time to read the entertainment news."

"Iron Thunder is, from all we can uncover, a high-tech death cult. Their adherents use file-sharing technology to stay in touch and spread their nihilist, hedonist, death-to-the-world, free-yourself-from-earthly-pain message. They've grown remarkably in just the last two years, leveraging the popularity of worldwide video clip and social networking sites. Their leader, the Jim Jones to this happy little Internet Jonestown, is a man named Helmut Schribner. Schribner calls himself Dumar Eon."

"Anything on him?"

"Not really," Brognola said. "A few minor investigations for cybercrimes, bank fraud, that kind of thing. Nothing that stuck. One abortive investigation into production of pornography, a local obscenity rap that escalated because he was transmitting the material on the Web. No convictions. Schribner, or 'Eon,' is smart, technically savvy and very charismatic. He's the Pied Piper here. If the online posts are any indication, his followers are devoted, and dangerously so."

"That sort of thing usually leads to worse, sooner or later," Bolan said. "Like the skinhead in California who attacked that interracial couple. The group he said gave him the idea got sued into bankruptcy. This cult see anything like that?"

"Nothing criminal," Brognola said. "They've skirted the other side of the law a few times, officially, and been the target of at least one lawsuit in the United States because a high-school kid committed suicide after watching a bunch of their video clips. On the whole, though, nothing is traceable to them that would prompt more serious legal intervention."

"How are they tied to the Consortium?" Bolan asked.

"One of the recent 'accidents' befell a man named Hermann Gruebner, owner and CEO of something called Arbeit Technopolitik. It's a small company that makes printed circuit cards that eventually find their way into military equipment. Gruebner was supposedly mugged and strangled by a drug addict while jogging early one morning. Happened a couple of months ago. His mugger was stabbed in prison after a fast-track trial and conviction. The company, of course, was sold in the wake of his tragic death. We've traced the new owners to the Consortium."

"Tidy," Bolan said.

"Too tidy," Brognola agreed. "Bear's team ran a background check on the mugger, including known aliases off- and online, and they got a bunch of hits for videos uploaded to a popular video sharing and social networking site. All of them were Iron Thunder clips—proselytizing for the cult."

"So a member of a German underground techno-death-cult murdered this CEO for reasons unknown, and took those reasons to an early grave at the end of a shank."

"Exactly," Brognola said. "Once we had that, and knew what to look for, we were able to turn up several more hits, some solid, some tenuous. Many of the accidents can be linked to persons with ties to Iron Thunder. It looks as if the Consortium is using the cult as street muscle to do the dirty work, clear the way for these strategic takeovers where necessary. Some purchases go down completely aboveboard. Some are problematic, and any obstacles are mysteriously and quickly removed, permanently. We figure they're using a tried-and-true combination of bribery, influence peddling, intimidation and outright murder when needed."

"And so the Consortium gobbles up business after business."

"Yes," Brognola said. "And that's the problem. All the while it's doing so, it's trying to hide what's going on. And that tells me, and the Man, that the Consortium is making a play for control of Germany's strategic industries. Whether for pure profit, selling war matériel to the highest bidder, or out of some agenda to help hostile nations, we don't know. The outcome is more or less the same. Whether terrorists or rogue nations that sponsor terrorists, Germany's industries form key links in the global technology chain. If Germany falls behind the scenes, it puts the United States and the rest of the Western world in peril."

"Why me, then, Hal?" Bolan asked. "What is SOG's interest in this? Sounds like a job for more…mainstream government agencies."

"It would be," Brognola said, "if we had anything that the international law enforcement community would consider solid proof. We've got leads, correlations and damning circumstantial evidence, all of it turned up through mostly extralegal computer searches and traces run by Bear and his team. None of it is enough to convince the powers that be that official action is necessary."

"What about the German government?" Bolan asked.

"As far as it's concerned," Brognola said, "this isn't happening. The Consortium is a good domestic company and therefore trustworthy, officially. Whether the Germans are blind to what's going on or just trying to cover their collective backsides, we don't know. But they're not happy that we've even raised the question. I spent several hours on the phone through channels, pulling strings and busting heads. They don't like it, but they've reluctantly agreed to allow what is officially being considered an Interpol investigation."

"Interpol?" Bolan asked.

"It gets us in the door," Brognola said. "It doesn't matter who they think we are, as long as you can get in and get it done. Basically, the Man wants you to go in and fix this problem. If you can get proof and we can secure further international cooperation, or direct cooperation with the Germans, that's fine. If you can't, you can still do what you do, burn them out and down, and put an end to this threat. Those are the President's instructions."

"Why not simply go to the source, then? We eliminate the Consortium and its heads. Problem solved, except for some mop-up of the cult."

"Won't work," Brognola said. "The Consortium closely guards its membership rolls. We don't know who they are, though we suspect in many cases. There are maybe three or four executives we could put you on, but that won't begin to solve the problem. You need to find out who you're dealing with, on the ground, by following the slime trails back to their source."

"I'm a soldier, not a detective, Hal."

"I'm not asking you to detect," Brognola said. "I'm asking you to perform reconnaissance, then search and destroy."

"Understood."

"Let the Germans and Interpol think you're who we tell them, unless and until you identify your targets. Then work around to the enemy, regardless."

"Just how hostile will the locals be to my presence?"

"Officially, we're letting them believe you're one of the blacker sheep within the CIA," Brognola said. "You'll get nominal support and lip service, but don't expect open arms."

"Business as usual, then," Bolan said.

"Yes," the big Fed went on. "It doesn't end there. In order to get local cooperation we've agreed to let Interpol assign us a contact. The Man himself secured their consent to work with us on this. They've been made aware of the broad strokes, or at least a sanitized version of them, though they have no idea who is behind this in truth."

"Of course," Bolan said.

"Stand by," Brognola told him. "I'm transmitting you the contact's dossier now. He's relatively green, but nevertheless attached to one of the more shadowy branches of the Agency and its German equivalent. Born to German and American parents, educated here in the States. Did a few years abroad and in the Army, all of it post–iron curtain."

"Can we trust him?"

"As far as we can trust anybody," Brognola said. "Interpol thinks it's taking the lead on this issue now, and we're happy to let it. It allows us to operate under its umbrella, since we don't officially exist. Your contact may even produce some worthwhile leads, or relay what Interpol manages to produce between now and when you hit ground in Germany."

"All right, then," Bolan had agreed. "I guess I'd better get going."

"I guess you better," Brognola had replied. "Good hunting, Striker."

"Right." Bolan had closed the connection.

Now, hours later, Bolan and Rieck sat facing each other over the dossier Interpol had managed to put together, and which Rieck had turned over. Bolan nodded, finally, jerking his chin toward the photographs and looking at Rieck. To his credit, the man understood without being told that Bolan wanted a synopsis.

"That," Rieck said, indicating a photograph, "is Hans Becker, the president of Becker Aerospace. BA produces key missile guidance systems. It's considered a prime 'get' in strategic industrial circles, and in the last several months it's been having financial problems. An accidental warehouse fire here, a few key developers lost to a car accident there. Word is it's ripe for buyout, but Becker, who owns the controlling interest, is resisting. It's a family-owned company and always has been."

"A prime target, in other words," Bolan nodded. Watching the doorway from his seat, he saw a trio of young people, possibly students, wearing disposable plastic ponchos. Two of them had backpacks slung over one shoulder.

"Yes," Rieck said. "Our analysts predict that BA is the most probable object of the Consortium's interests. It's financially vulnerable, it produces a strategically critical line of components, and Becker has reported some harassment to the local authorities."

"Harassment?"

"Being followed, some late-night hang-up calls, and a few incidents of vandalism at his home here in Berlin," Rieck said, pulling a hard copy of a digital photograph from the stack. The building it depicted appeared to be an apartment or condominium high-rise, its architecture a blend of old-world charm and modern efficiency. It looked pricey, if Bolan was any judge. It was, in other words, just the sort of place a president or CEO would call home in this German city.

"And BA itself?" Bolan asked. The students he had noticed before, a young man and two women, were settling at a table by the corner. One woman was blond, the other brunette. The blonde in particular was a striking Norse beauty. Bolan had seen plenty of beautiful women in his unending war against terror. He'd seen more than a few who had been pretty *before* the predators got done with them, too. It was a sobering thought.

"Offices here, on Reinickendorfer Strasse," Rieck said, "and a secondary manufacturing facility maybe an hour from the city, in Muencheberg."

"Were does Becker spend his time?"

"The accidental deaths of some of his contemporaries in the high-tech field here in Germany haven't gone unnoticed to Becker," Rieck said, as if he and Bolan were sharing a very important secret. "He's been holed up in his suite for the last week, and we know he has employed a bodyguard agency here in the city. They're expensive, thoroughly licensed and heavily armed."

"Your recommendation?" Bolan asked, ignoring Rieck's conspiratorial tone.

"I would start with Muencheberg," Rieck said. "If Becker's holdings are being monitored, we might be able to find some of the operatives responsible. We might even catch them in the act of vandalizing Becker's property. These incidents have increased sharply in the past several days. There have been three reports in the last week alone."

"It's a start," Bolan said. "But if Becker is the target, it's Becker we should begin with. He's the key. Removing him removes the primary obstacle to the Consortium's acquisition of his company. If they orchestrated the problems that have put BA in deep, which it's likely they have, it makes even more sense that they're setting him up for a heavy fall."

"But he's guarded," Rieck said. "Won't that keep him out of play for now?"

"I've never known it to mean much in the past," Bolan said. "Hired guards are hired guards. They're good as far as they go. But his apartment is no fortress. How could it be? I've seen hard targets, Rieck. This won't qualify."

"Well, all right," Rieck began, "but I don't see why—"

The beautiful blonde at the table in the corner reached into her backpack. Bolan was watching her out of the corner of his eye. When her arm came up with a micro-Uzi submachine gun in her small fist, he had just enough time to register the threat. He put one hand against the table and pushed off.

Automatic gunfire ripped through the coffee shop.

2

"Down!" Bolan roared, throwing himself back and off his chair. Rieck reacted quickly and hit the floor. The burst of bullets went wide but stitched the wall behind and between the two men nonetheless. Rieck would have been dead had he stayed seated a fraction of a second longer.

Screams erupted as the coffee shop's customers registered what was happening. Suddenly the shop was full of running, hysterical men and women, shouting in at least three languages.

Rieck upended the table and crouched behind its dubious cover, drawing his four-inch Smith & Wesson. Bolan had seen this type of scenario go down more than once, and knew that hiding or playing a time-compressed waiting game simply wouldn't work. With each passing second, the risk that an innocent civilian would be hit increased. He pulled the Beretta 93-R from its custom leather shoulder rig, flipped the selector to single shot and brought the snout of the evil-looking little machine pistol on target. Then he charged forward, moving left, then right, crouching low, being careful not to put innocents into the line of fire by getting between them and the shooters. The Beretta led the way, and as he charged, Bolan fired.

The desperate offensive took the momentum from the attackers. The Executioner had seen that sudden look of confusion before, the instant when an enemy, having visualized the killing time and again, suddenly locked up or froze when confronted with something unexpected. These shooters were the hunters, in their minds; they had come to deal death. They didn't expect to see death hurtling back at them. The enemy broke under the onslaught, scattering. Bolan caught the blonde with the Uzi first.

She was trying to swing her submachine gun onto him when Bolan reached her, slamming a brutal elbow up and across her chin, knocking her sprawling. The Uzi slid from nerveless fingers as she went down and out. The man, not as young as his college dress had made him seem from a distance, had drawn a small automatic pistol from under his clothes and was taking aim. Bolan put a single 9 mm bullet between his eyes, and he collapsed to the floor of the coffee shop.

The third shooter, the other woman, screamed as she traded fire with Rieck. The Interpol agent's shots were truer, clipping her in the arm and sending her screaming to the ground. Bolan scooped up the revolver she'd been carrying, turned and stood over her, the Beretta aimed at her head.

"Do *not* move," he ordered.

Rieck, coming up to stand behind him, said something in German, which Bolan understood to be the same instructions. The young woman, pretty enough, with dark, naturally curly hair and fine-boned features, looked at them with such hatred that her face became a mask of ugly evil. She cursed in German. Bolan spared a glance at Rieck.

"She says you will know everlasting peace," Rieck said, nonplussed.

"That's a new one," Bolan said. "Let's get this mopped up."

Rieck proved his worth, barking orders, taking immediate charge of the chaotic scene. His Interpol credentials got a workout as he directed the customers to sit and calm down, while ordering the nearest shop attendant to call the appropriate authorities. Bolan, meanwhile, secured the two women with plastic zip-tie cuffs, searched them and then searched the corpse. He found nothing useful. There were only a few personal items like combs and brushes, a small folding knife in the dead man's pocket, and extra ammunition for the weapons they carried. Bolan unloaded and set aside the Uzi, the dead man's ancient Colt .380 automatic pistol, and the Smith & Wesson snub nose the wounded woman had tried to use.

Flashing blue lights outside alerted the men to the approach of the local police. "There they are," Rieck said, rising to look over the shell-shocked customers one last time. He nodded to Bolan. "I'll make sure that ambulance is on the way." There was no telling how many of the shop's customers were suffering shock. Routine medical treatment was needed as part of containing the shooting and its aftermath.

The front door of the coffee shop opened again.

The men who entered, dressed in dark suits, carried Heckler & Koch MP-5 submachine guns. The man in the lead raised his weapon at Rieck. The killing intent in his eyes was unmistakable. This wasn't backup.

Rieck went for his gun, but there was no way he would make it in time. Death waited for him in the chamber of the lead shooter's MP-5.

Bolan's Desert Eagle thundered.

The .44 Magnum hollowpoint round took the gunner in the face, rocking him back. The gunner behind him faltered as he watched his partner suddenly go down, and Bolan shot him neatly through the neck. Yelling for Rieck to get down— the agent obligingly flattened himself—the big American emptied the Desert Eagle's magazine through the doorway, targeting the silver Mercedes parked at the curb outside. The heavy rounds punched through the passenger-side front tire and fender, skimming across the hood and driving another gunner to cover behind the engine block.

"Go, go!" Bolan directed. Rieck scrambled forward, snatched up the Uzi Bolan had taken from the blonde, and slammed its magazine home on the move. Unbidden, the Interpol agent broke right while Bolan broke left, both men pushing through the doors and into the nighttime hellstorm outside.

The soldier quickly assessed the scenario. There were two vehicles, both silver Mercedes. He quickly counted targets. There were a half-dozen men, at least, moving in and around the cars, weapons at the ready. He ducked and dodged aside, Rieck mirroring his movements, as gunfire struck the windows behind them. There were more screams from within the coffee shop. Bolan snapped his gaze back long enough to confirm that the customers were on the floor, out of the direct line of fire. Grimly, he ripped the Beretta from its holster, both pistols in his fists now as he aimed first the Desert Eagle, then the Beretta, and pulled the triggers.

The 3-round burst from the Beretta 93-R caught the nearest shooter as he bobbed up from behind the engine block of the shot-up Mercedes. The man went down with a burst through his throat. Then the Executioner was up and over, throwing himself across the hood of the car. He came down on the other side next to the dead man, surprising two shooters crouched in the open driver's doors.

One of the men got off a shot that went wide as Bolan triggered a .44 round through his face. At the same moment, the Beretta 93-R barked, punching a 3-round burst through the heart of the second man. Both gunners went slack in their seats.

The unmistakable chatter of an Uzi, so familiar a sound to Bolen after years on international battlefields, erupted from behind the second vehicle. Rieck was crouched low and moving smoothly behind the rear of the car. He was canted slightly forward, leaning into the submachine gun, triggering short, controlled bursts. It was textbook mechanics for such a

weapon. Bolan raised his mental estimation of the agent once
more; the man thought clearly enough under fire to recover
the terrorist weapon and use it to good effect, and he obviously had the training to do it properly. Rieck's 9 mm bursts
dropped two more of the suited shooters.

The last two men—no, three, Bolan revised, as a third man
came from around the corner of the coffee shop and ran for
the street—began to withdraw, covering each other in turn
with their weapons. The suppressing fire from first one, then
the other MP-5 pushed Bolan and Rieck back down behind
the two Mercedes sedans.

Bolan went prone, rolling into position under the middle
of his car. He placed the Beretta on the pavement and aimed
the Desert Eagle with both hands, targeting the retreating,
then running men. These would be difficult shots.

There was no better marksman than the Executioner.

The first .44 slug caught the trailing shooter in the ankle.
He screamed and fell, rolling on the wet pavement. The MP-5
was still in his fists, so Bolan dealt him a shot to the head.

The soldier's third bullet caught the middle runner in mid-
calf. He folded over without a sound, almost somersaulting
as he lost his footing. Bolan could hear his skull crack on the
pavement.

Bolan's fourth bullet took the farthest gunner in one thigh.
He stumbled and nearly fell, but somehow managed to keep
moving. The momentary crouch was all the Executioner
needed. He snapped another long-distance shot into the man's
head. The body hit the sidewalk on the far side of the street,
a crumpled heap beside a storm drain.

Rieck popped up and brought the Uzi forward. He stalked
ahead, just a few steps at a time, scanning the surrounding
area. Bolan did the same, watching his side while the Interpol
agent covered the other. They moved around the cars once,
then again, checking to make sure all of the new shooters had
been taken.

"Clear!" Rieck called.

"Clear," Bolan stated. He checked once more, then reloaded and holstered the Desert Eagle. The Beretta 93-R he reloaded but kept at the ready.

"Start checking bodies," he instructed Rieck. "I'll see if we've got any live ones." Specifically, he was interested in the gunner who'd hit his head. It was possible he was still alive. Bolan checked the other two first, confirming they were dead, then knelt next to the man in question. He fingered the neck for a pulse and then rolled the body over.

The man stared back, eyes lifeless and glassy. Bolan could tell from the angle the head lolled that the shooter had broken his neck in the fall. Bolan swore. He'd hoped for a live enemy to interrogate, but that couldn't be helped. Searching through the man's pockets, he found an extra magazine for the MP-5 in the suit jacket. There was also a fixed-blade fighting knife strapped inside the dead man's waistband at the small of his back. He carried nothing else. No identification. Bolan left the knife where it was and stood. Rieck was quietly and efficiently going through the other dead men's pockets.

In the distance, the seesaw foghorn of German police sirens could be heard. The legitimate German authorities were responding, either to Rieck's calls or to the sounds of gunfire. Bolan saw civilians, bystanders, poking their heads out from behind improvised cover: a man behind a kiosk here, a woman with two small children, out late, hiding in a doorway there. Keeping these people from the cross fire was the primary reason he had brought hell to the enemy, yet again.

Rieck looked mildly wild-eyed. He shucked the empties from his Smith & Wesson—a .357 Magnum, Bolan noted—and popped in a speedloader of fresh rounds.

"Did you find anything?" he asked.

"No." Bolan shook his head. "You?"

Rieck held out a single laminated ID card. It bore credentials in German, with a photo ID. The name Sicherheit Vereinigung.

"The Security Consortium." Bolan looked up at Rieck.

"Do you think those three in the shop—"

"No," Bolan said. "Not likely, anyway."

"I don't understand what happened," Rieck said. "First those three in the shop, and then this group."

"Assassins," Bolan said. "That much is obvious. The first three were amateurs. Vicious, but amateurs. These—" he nodded to the bodies of the shooters from the Mercedes "—are professionals. The Consortium sent its hired guns after you. Somebody wants you dead, Rieck."

"But how? And why?"

"You had to have been followed," Bolan said.

"I could believe I was followed by those three kids," Rieck said. "They'd blend in easily enough. But three kids and a parade of Mercedes sedans full of professional soldiers? I may not have your experience, Cooper, but I'm not *that* stupid."

"All right." Bolan nodded. "These Consortium shooters' involvement remains an unknown. But suddenly you're very popular."

"How do you know it was me, and not you?"

"Well," Bolan said, "you're the only person locally who even knew to meet me. I find it hard to believe my mission has been blown completely so quickly. That girl with the Uzi targeted you first, too."

"You *saw* that?"

"I see everything," Bolan said dismissively. "That's not the point. Those 'kids' were obviously after you, so they must have been following you, unless someone else knew where we'd be meeting. It's the only logical answer."

"No," Rieck said. "I picked the shop myself and had your people relay it. I assume you trust them and their communications?"

"Absolutely," Bolan said. There was no way his secure satellite phone or Stony Man Farm's scrambled up- and down-links could be compromised, at least at this stage of the game. If the Consortium already knew he was here, and where to find him, the mission was over before it had started. He didn't think that likely, though he'd been party to plenty of operations in which everything that could go wrong had.

"Did anyone else at Interpol locally know to whom you'd been assigned, or why?" Bolan asked.

"A few," Rieck admitted. "I'd hate to think we have a leak in the agency."

"You might," Bolan said. "That, too, is the simplest explanation."

"Well, we'll see about that," Rieck said. "Once they've been checked by the medics we'll get those two women across the table in an interrogation room and see if we can get them to tell us anything." They had reached the front of the coffee shop. Rieck put his hand out, swinging the door open.

He stopped. Somewhere in the corner of the shop, one of the witnesses was sobbing. Another man began to protest loudly in German. Bolan didn't know the words, but he knew the tone: *Hey, man, it wasn't me, I didn't do anything.*

"Jesus," Rieck said. The toe of his shoe was red with blood.

Bolan pushed past him and checked first one, then the other prisoner. He didn't blame the bystanders for not interfering. Chances were, they'd been unaware of precisely what they were seeing until it was too late. Only a few minutes' inattention, while Bolan and Rieck were contending with the new shooters, was all the captured shooters had needed. The two women had pushed themselves together on the floor, presumably after the blonde had regained consciousness. Then the two of them had evidently opened each other's necks...with their teeth.

"Sweet mother of…" Rieck muttered. "Cooper, what could inspire such an act?"

Bolan looked down at the two dead women, adding the ghastly scene to the too-long catalog in his mind.

"Are they?" Rieck asked.

"Yeah," Bolan said. "They are."

The sirens outside grew louder. Rieck checked, his hand on his gun, ready for anything. "The police and two ambulances. Too late for them, I guess." He nodded to the dead women.

Bolan shook his head. He'd seen plenty of fanatics willing to kill or die for their cause. Call it a gut instinct, but these women didn't seem to be the type to take their lives for an abstract slogan. No, rather than a cause, rather than a vague "what," this type of brutal self-sacrifice was most often, in Bolan's experience, committed for a "who."

So Rieck's question stood. They'd have to answer it, too, because it was central to the battle they now fought. This force, this entity, this malevolent being, stood at the center of the maelstrom of violence now threatening to storm across Germany. They needed to know, sooner rather than later.

Just who could inspire this kind of bloodshed?

3

The man known to followers worldwide as Dumar Eon leaned back in his swiveling office chair, steepling his fingers as he stared out the grimy window to the rain-soaked nighttime streets of Berlin. The distant traffic, its rattle and roar incessant and rhythmic, was like a heartbeat. Often he listened to the city, this delightfully sick, this terminally ill city, and fancied he would be there on the day that Berlin's heart stopped forever.

The austere and immaculately clean office was incongruous in the otherwise decrepit building it occupied. This was the heart of the worst, most crime-ridden, most crumbling section of Berlin's Neukölln neighborhood. Dumar Eon had heard of Neukölln referred to as a "dynamic" and even "vibrant" suburb, and he supposed there were portions of it that could be considered that. The Neukölln *he* knew, however, was considerably more deadly than anyone might see written up in real estate periodicals.

Eon stood and went to the window, which was covered with dust. The rain and the headlights of passing vehicles on the narrow streets all but obscured the view, but he peered out placidly as if he could see every crack in the mortar of the surrounding structures. The vaguely L-shaped building, a throwback to the older European architecture of this part of the neighborhood, squatted miserably on a bustling corner, boarded windows like broken or missing teeth marring its otherwise graffiti-covered facade.

The heavy walnut desk that dominated the room was worth more than the building itself, he imagined. It was covered with multiple flat-screen monitors, not to mention a webcam and microphone. Behind the desk, centered in the webcam's frame, was the black-and-white banner of Iron Thunder: a sledgehammer and a stylized chainsaw in white silhouette on the black field. Thus did the ranks of Iron Thunder smash and clear-cut all those who stood in their way, all those who refused to accept their message. Dumar Eon was well aware that the iconography was slightly less than timeless, but that didn't matter. Iron Thunder was a religion for today, for the technology of today, and like a shark, it would have to keep moving forward if it wasn't to die.

Of course, death was the ultimate message of Iron Thunder, the goal toward which they all worked, the gift they sought to bring others. Certainly, the sect was also devoted to the pleasures of the flesh, to the indulgence of all worldly desires, for as long as the curse of life was inflicted on each adherent. But the final purity, the cleansing toward which all Iron Thunder followers marched, was of course the sweet oblivion of nonexistence. No afterlife, no heavenly reward, no eternal damnation—only the long, endless expanse of peace that was *not to be*. Eon thought to himself that, were he not so very busy bringing Iron Thunder's message to the world, he might take the revolver from his desk drawer and put it in his mouth right now. He smiled at the thought, knowing that eternal release was only a few pounds of trigger pressure away at any moment.

This was, of course, the tightrope he and all of Iron Thunder's believers walked, though he was much more keenly aware of it than were they. Daily, weekly, monthly, the problem that Dumar Eon faced was simple enough: How could he keep Iron Thunder's ranks growing, convince those within those ranks that death was the highest ideal, yet forestall their suicides for as long as possible in order to further Iron Thunder's work? He supposed that was the sacrifice that all great men, all leaders, endured each day. The greatest saints never knew the blessings they brought to others, so busy were they doing the work that conferred those blessings.

Eon folded his hands behind his back and continued to stare out the window. He cut an imposing figure as he did so. He was tall, an inch over six feet. He wore a tailored black suit, pressed white shirt and matching black silk tie. His shoes were Italian imports, as were the black leather gloves on his hands. The black, wire-rimmed sunglasses he wore, even now, cost nearly as much as the shoes, and were preferred among international film stars and other luminaries. Above a clean-shaved, strong-jawed, chiseled-chinned face just starting to show the hint of five-o'clock shadow, Eon wore his lustrous black hair straight to his shoulders, maintained by weekly visits to an exclusive and obscenely priced Berlin salon.

The revolver in Eon's desk was an expensive, engraved .357 Magnum Korth with a four-inch barrel. The watch on his wrist was a Rolex. The wallet in his jacket held nothing but a fake ID and an equally fake passport, while the money clip in Eon's pants was gold-plated and crammed with a small fortune in euros.

Life, for Dumar Eon, was good.

Death would be better. But it would wait.

With a wistful sigh, he returned to his desk, and to the state-of-the-art computer and satellite Internet connection that waited for him.

The multiple monitors were all linked to the same PC. Dumar paused to take in the charts and scrolling figures that represented his various stock holdings. He frowned as he compared New York to Tokyo. He took a moment to fire off an encrypted e-mail to one of his brokers, stipulating a pair of stocks to dump on the TSE. Then, casting a baleful eye over the NASDAQ and assessing, mentally, the implications of an impending commodities report—the streaming video from the world's largest cable news network appeared as a picture-in-picture window on his right-hand monitor—the man born as Helmut Schribner tapped a few entries into his record-keeping spreadsheet.

His holdings continued to grow. It was a fundamental principle of investing that he who has money can make more of it relatively easily. Helmut Schribner's experience had proved no exception to that rule. Born into a poor family in Stuttgart, he had once thought to end his days as little more than he had started them—a line worker in a screen printing shop. He had always known ambition, but lacked the tools, the direction, to channel it. Thus did Helmut Schribner live his life day to day in a state of dissatisfaction, a vague unease.

Every day he would leave the printing shop and spend what precious little disposable income he had at a pub around the block. He hadn't yet learned, in those days, to mask his feelings. Clearly, then, his thoughts had shown on this face, for one day a man sat next to him and told him those thoughts.

"You," the stranger said in accented but fluent German, "are not happy."

Helmut Schribner eventually learned that this man, in his late fifties and born in England, was named Phineas Elmington. Elmington was a British expatriate. He alluded to some crime he had committed, something for which he'd fled England. Schribner assumed that the name "Phineas Elmington" was an alias. It hardly mattered. For whatever reason, Elmington, a sadist and a sociopath, saw some manner of kindred spirit in Schribner. The more they talked over their beers, the more both men came to realize that.

"You are not happy," Elmington said to him. "You live wondering what should be different. You live wondering what should be your purpose. You come here and drink away your money because you do not know what else to do."

Schribner had to admit that this man was right. As they spoke at length, night after night, discovering they shared common perspectives on the world around them, Elmington's questions grew bolder and more direct.

"Look around you, Helmut," he said one fateful evening. "Do you see your fellow men? Do you wish to cherish them and help them? Serve them? Or do you see so many insects, so many irrelevancies? Do you see men or do you see bags of meat?"

"Bags of meat," Schribner had answered without hesitation.

"You have always hated them, haven't you?" Elmington asked. "I could see it in your eyes before I first spoke to you. You hate them as I do."

"I…I suppose I do," Schribner admitted.

"And you would kill them, if you could."

Schribner looked at the Englishman, eyes widening. "Why…yes. Yes, I would. It would be nothing."

"It would be nothing to you," Elmington nodded. "That is what I saw in your eyes. That is what you can be."

"What do you mean?" Schribner asked.

"I want you to kill me," Elmington said.

It hadn't been as preposterous as it first sounded. Elmington revealed that he was dying. It was cancer of the pancreas, and he had perhaps months. He had learned all that only a few weeks earlier, a single day before approaching Schribner in the pub.

"I find, as I stare into the face of death," Elmington said, "that it is a gift. It is the greatest gift. It is peace. It is oblivion. I wish to have this gift, now, before my suffering grows great.

I have always known that it was a gift one could give to others, but now I wish to have it for myself. You may be the one to give it to me, I think."

"I suppose…I suppose I could." Schribner licked his lips at the thought. He found the idea intriguing, even exciting.

"To kill is no small thing," Elmington warned. "It requires a mind like iron. You must have a hard will to withstand the storm. For when death comes, it does not come quietly, no matter how silently the victim dies. No, when death comes, it rolls across you like thunder, and leaves behind only those touched by its gift—and of course those left alive to witness its passing."

Like a moth to a flame, like a man hypnotized, Schribner followed Elmington to the man's flat in Stuttgart. There, at an ancient rolltop desk, Elmington removed several ledgers from a drawer and placed them in Schribner's hands.

"These are my account books," he said. "They contain everything required to access their contents. Account numbers, passwords, balances. Special conditions of the concealment of various funds. I want you to have it."

"What is all this?" Schribner asked, looking down at the notebooks in his hands.

"The accumulation of a life's work," Elmington said. "Passed on to you, in reward for the gift you are about to bestow."

"I don't know what to say," Schribner murmured. He placed the ledgers on the nearby end table. Elmington was searching through the top drawer of his desk and finally produced a pistol.

"This is a Luger," Elmington said. He pulled on a portion of the pistol at its rear, causing some sort of toggle to flip out and back from the top. "It dates to World War II. It is in perfect working order. I have placed a round in the chamber. Take it, but be very careful. Do not touch the trigger."

Schribner took the weapon gingerly. Elmington positioned himself on the settee, propping a pillow under his head. He took the second throw pillow and gestured with it.

"I am going to place this over my head," he said. "I want you to put the barrel of the gun to the middle of the pillow and pull the trigger twice."

"All right," Schribner nodded. He felt strangely at ease with this act.

"Thank you," Elmington said. He placed the pillow over his head.

The shots were muffled. Elmington trembled once and then was still. Schribner stood over him for a long time, just watching him, before he realized that were the police to be alerted, he would be caught and taken away for murder. Gathering up the ledgers, he left, careful not to run lest he draw attention.

It took him a few days to go through everything Elmington had given him. When he was ready, he went to one of the new Internet cafés and began accessing the accounts. As he did so, his face grew hot. He couldn't believe just how much money Elmington had. It was a small fortune, enough to keep him in beer for the next two decades, or enough to build a much greater fortune, if wisely invested.

Before he realized what was happening, Helmut Schribner spent twelve hours at the computer. He didn't eat. He didn't move. Only when he realized just how badly he needed to use the restroom did he come up for air. By then, he knew what lay before him.

Helmut Schribner, previously at a loss for focus, had finally found two. The first, as he educated himself on finance and investing, moving from Web site to Web site, from resource to resource, was money. With the funds available to him, Schribner could build true wealth.

The second focus for Schribner's life came quite unexpectedly. He was intensely curious as to the history of his sudden benefactor. None of the account names he had received, of those that bore names at all, carried the name Phineas Elmington. When he searched this identity on the Internet, he discovered why. "Phineas Elmington" was a rather notorious English serial killer.

The news photos he was able to find showed that Elmington had changed his face, somehow, prior to going into hiding. There were various subtle differences, but it was clear that the man Schribner had shot was indeed the man wanted for multiple grisly murders in Great Britain. Schribner read everything he could about the case. Elmington's victims had nothing in common, nor did Elmington's murders share many traits to connect them. This had allowed him to become one of the most prolific serial killers in history. He had attacked men, women, children, the elderly…basically, anyone who happened to cross his path during the course of his life. He had strangled them, stabbed them, shot them, bludgeoned them, crushed them with furniture and, once, burned an entire apartment building just to see how many people wouldn't get out. When finally caught, he had told the authorities he wasn't a murderer at all, but a man bringing the gift of peace to those whose lives he took. He had been tried, but before he could be sentenced, he had disappeared from prison. Three guards died during the escape. Phineas Elmington had never been heard from again. The hunt for him had obsessed Great Britain for a time, but eventually it had been called off, and Elmington was believed, perhaps, to have taken his own life, based on some of the writings found in his home in London. Those writings had extolled the virtues, the blessing, of death.

When, during his search for information on Elmington, Schribner had found videos on a video-sharing Web site devoted to the man, he was both surprised and mesmerized. It seemed there was no shortage of devotees to so famous a murderer, and he found more than one video clip that either paid a kind of homage to Elmington—or other killers like him—or professed an outright admiration. Many of those

sitting before low-quality webcams proclaiming their obses-
sion with death and killing were young people, some costumed
in various goth outfits and makeup. They were from all walks
of life, apparently, and from all over the world.

It was then that Helmut Schribner had the idea that would
become the second focus for his life, and what he would come
to consider his true mission, his real purpose. The money he
would make, the money he would use, would be a means to
this end. For as he stared at the flickering, sometimes blurry,
always hypnotic images on the monitor, he realized just how
much power there was in this virtual environment, how much
value there was in being able to reach out through the computer to touch lives and those who lived them all around the
planet.

Having spent so much of his own life merely waiting for
something to happen, Schribner could be very patient. He did
his homework, studying fully the medium he planned to use
to execute his plan. Phineas Elmington had shown him the
way. When Schribner had pulled the trigger of that pistol, he
had known a sense of satisfaction, even of pleasure, that was
unlike anything he had previously experienced. He yearned
to feel it again, and more, to share it with others. He would
use this new and marvelous worldwide Web to spread his
message, to gain converts to what he could only describe as a
religion. A religion of death. A religion of oblivion. A religion
of ultimate pleasure.

As he studied, and as he began to notice the fanciful names
and nicknames used by those who created accounts on the
file-sharing sites he visited, Schribner realized that the task
before him wasn't one for a "Helmut Schribner." No, he would
require a new name, one that held within it a hint of the future,
one that concealed his past while showing the way ahead. He
thought, very briefly, about adopting Phineas Elmington's

name, but that wouldn't do. Elmington's time was past, and to appropriate his name seemed almost disrespectful to his legacy.

Looking through the ledgers, Helmut found it.

One of the account names in the ledger, one of the pseudonyms—many of them almost gibberish, nonsense words that Elmington had used as placeholders to keep the accounts separate—was "Dumar Eon." He liked it; "Dumar" sounded vaguely German, while "Eon" held a hint of timelessness. It was, simply put, the name of someone who could lead others, the name of someone who could share the gift, and the giving of that gift, that Phineas Elmington had demonstrated and experienced.

And so Helmut Schribner became Dumar Eon.

The name of the organization he would eventually form, in order to give Elmington's gift and his cause an identity that lent itself to marketing, he took from Elmington's own words: Iron Thunder.

In the coming months and then years, Dumar Eon learned he had a natural gift for marketing, an intuitive showmanship. He spread the word of Iron Thunder's beliefs, which he codified on several anonymous Web sites. Like a virus, word of Iron Thunder grew among those receptive to its message. The appeal of the sect cut across demographics, reaching something primal.

All the while, Dumar Eon's fortune grew.

Through shrewd, patient, long-term investing, Eon managed to multiply his start-up funding tenfold, then a hundredfold, then beyond. It was, therefore, only a matter of time, as he grew more educated in such matters, that Eon thought to create a German investment fund of his own. He located men and women he could trust, people who, even if they were not members of Iron Thunder, were either sympathetic to his cause or so blinded by desire for money that they cared little what he did. These he put in charge of the corporate face and broadening ventures of his new Security Consortium. And he implemented his long-term plan: to use the resources of the Consortium, first to gain control of certain very important industries in Germany, and then to funnel the matériel produced thereby to those international entities who could—however unwittingly—continue to carry the gift of death.

It had worked so well. The Consortium had grown larger than any one person could manage, and he put the appropriate individuals in place to run it. He had made sure to choose only those who valued secrecy, who safeguarded their identities, as did he. If he chose his most trusted operatives from among the shadows, they would remain within them. Thus they all had something to lose if they were exposed, and all would look to their own interests and preserve the whole.

Recently he had, as was only expected, become aware of the Interpol investigation. It paid to have the right people in the right places. To preserve Iron Thunder, it was necessary to stop the investigation before it began. And so he had dispatched the appropriate personnel. Eon imagined they were even now bringing peace to the would-be crime fighter Interpol had assigned. With the agent dead, the whole affair could be quietly covered up. A little push here, some thoughtfully used influence there, perhaps a bribe or two. The authorities could be bought, or otherwise contained. An object lesson now and then helped keep them in check. As for his own organization, the killing of a single bureaucratic drone, or even a swarm of them, would draw little attention.

Over time he had learned that, except for those true believers from among the ranks of Iron Thunder, very few of the people running the Consortium cared what went on, where the money went, what the investment fund's ultimate goals were, or what actions were taken in pursuit of those goals. They cared only to fill their own pockets. Eon preferred that. It was predictable, and predictable quantities were quantities that could be managed and manipulated for his own purposes.

Those purposes were what truly mattered. Those purposes would be poorly understood by certain less…spiritual entities within the Consortium, and thus those entities didn't need to know what Dumar Eon really wanted.

In the long term, Dumar Eon sought to burn the world.

He wished to cleanse it with the fires of pure oblivion. He would, if he could, kill everyone and everything in and on it, everything moving across the face of the earth.

Eventually.

There really was no hurry. As he contemplated the finer things he had acquired and did enjoy, he thought that while the final and most blissful peace of death was undeniable, neither was there any reason to rush toward it.

There was so much work left to be done.

4

Adam Rieck drove the BMW, which Bolan gathered was a rental, bringing it smoothly to the curb a block away from the building that housed Becker's residence. Bolan got out and turned his back, using the interior of the car to discreetly check his weapons. It was dark and getting quite late, and there were no people on the street that they could see, but it always paid to assume unseen eyes were watching.

They had endured no small amount of bureaucratic wrangling from the local authorities. Rieck had been forced to phone his contacts at Interpol, which prompted several more calls back and forth before all the red tape was untangled. The police were none too happy to let Bolan and Rieck go, especially armed as they were. Bolan had seen it countless times before. When the lead started flying, those left standing were immediately assumed to be at fault in some way.

Rieck used his trench coat to shield the bulk of the 12-gauge Remington 870 shotgun he carried. He had begged, borrowed or otherwise obtained the weapon from one of the responding German police units; Bolan didn't know exactly how he'd managed it and didn't care. The Uzi and the other recovered weapons had of course been taken as evidence, and Bolan was happy to leave that cleanup to the local authorities.

He turned to face the entrance to the building, surveying the block and scanning the windows. He saw nothing. The street was unnaturally quiet. A dog barked, somewhere faraway. He watched an empty coffee cup roll in lazy semicircles back and forth, stirred by a strong night breeze, grime from the wet street clinging to paper. He looked left, then right again. Something was wrong. Something subtle…

"Rieck," he said, "do you smell that?"

"Smell what?" The Interpol operative paused and sniffed at the air. Then he caught it. "Smoke," he said.

"Move," Bolan commanded. He drew the Beretta 93-R and hit the front door, shoving the glass-and-metal barrier aside and covering the corridor beyond. Rieck followed. The two men covered each other in turns as they worked their way up the corridor. Bolan followed his nose, more concerned with clearing each space than in reaching Becker's dwelling.

They cleared the first floor without incident, but on the second, the smoke became a visible haze. At the stairwell exit to the third floor, they found a body sprawled in the doorway. The man wore a suit and stared blankly in death, his hand clutching a walkie-talkie.

"Becker's security," Rieck whispered.

Bolan nodded curtly and motioned for silence.

The double doors leading into Becker's condominium—his name and address were on a burnished plate mounted outside—had been smashed inward, possibly with a portable battering ram. The lights were out. Bolan, his Beretta pointed before him, tried a wall switch. There was no response; the power had probably been cut, either to the flat or to the building. The walls and floors were scorched and cloying smoke filled the air around them, but there were no fires evident.

"Homemade flash-bangs," Rieck whispered. "Sort of a poor man's incendiary charge. Burns hot, fast and bright, but often won't set a blaze." He looked around. "Lots of hardwood floors here. Not a lot of carpets. We're lucky the building's not on fire."

"We need to clear this area," Bolan said. "Now."

Rieck nodded. Bolan unclipped his SureFire Combatlight, bracing it under his gun hand as he flashed the ultrabright xenon lamp, always moving, the barrel of the Beretta ready to acquire targets. Rieck had a small LED light of his own; he held it against the shotgun's pump and did a passable job of checking his own side of the condominium. They found more dead men. Pools of blood, scorched furniture and empty brass shell casings were everywhere.

A voice shouted weakly in German from the last room of the apartment.

Rieck and Bolan hit the room high and low, respectively. The soldier kicked the door in and his Interpol counterpart followed with the shotgun. They found no resistance; there was only Hans Becker himself, secured to a chair in the center of the room, surrounded by three dead bodyguards in a room that had been largely untouched by the fast-burning charges that had scorched the rest of the condominium.

There was something strapped to his chest.

Becker looked at them, wild-eyed. He had been beaten; a livid bruise was spreading across his left cheek, and the eye on that side was bloodshot and partially swollen shut. He had been duct-taped to a straight-backed antique chair. He was barefoot, wearing slacks and shirtsleeves. He said something weakly in German, his voice faltering. Bolan imagined he'd shouted himself hoarse after his tormenters had left him like this.

"He says it's a bomb," Rieck reported.

The device was a shoebox-size oblong wrapped in layer after layer of the same duct tape that was holding Becker in place. Canvas straps ran from the box across Becker's shoulders and under his arms, attached to the box from the back by some unseen means. Bolan eyed it, hard, but didn't reach for it. Becker's eyes followed Bolan's.

"Eisen-Donner," Becker whispered.

"Iron Thunder." Bolan nodded. He bent to examine the bomb. Becker immediately became agitated and started hissing in rapid-fire German, shaking his head.

"He says they warned him it would go off if it was touched," Rieck stated. "He has been trying not to move, while crying for help. He wants to know if we could please summon the police, and begs that we not touch the bomb."

"He's going to be disappointed then," Bolan said grimly, bending to place his ear near Becker's chest. "This thing is ticking."

"Wouldn't it anyway?" Rieck asked.

Bolan looked up at him. "The only reason for there to be timing connected to an explosive, is to set it off after a predetermined interval."

"So it's ticking…." The Interpol agent said.

"Because it's going to explode," Bolan finished.

"Your call, Cooper," Rieck stated.

Bolan looked at the box, then at Becker. Without a word, he drew a dagger from his waistband. Then he spared a glance at the agent. "Get out of here, Rieck. Phone it in."

"You sure?"

"There's nothing you can do," the Executioner said. "I'll take this."

"We could wait for the bomb squad."

"We could if we knew how long we have," Bolan answered. "We don't. It's only in the movies that the bomb has a big red LED readout staring you in the face."

Rieck looked at him, then at Becker. "You could…I mean, it's not your responsibility. You could get to safety."

Bolan eyed him hard. "The hell it's not."

Rieck nodded. "Then I'll stay with you. You can't watch your own back and deal with this, too. We've no idea who might still be around. The people who did this might return to watch the fireworks. This apartment is not secured." With that he checked his shotgun and stood back a few paces.

Bolan again raised his mental estimation of the Interpol agent.

Becker began muttering in agitated German. The soldier didn't bother asking Rieck to translate; the executive was clearly convinced any tampering with the bomb would cause it to go off. He was probably right. But Mack Bolan would no more retreat to safety and watch an innocent man be blown to bits than he would pass a wounded stranger on the sidewalk. With that thought foremost in his mind, he hefted the dagger and got to work.

Using the keen edge of the compact fighting knife, Bolan made an incision around the oblong. The tape separated easily under the knife's tip. Then, very carefully, Bolan peeled back the square of tape, making sure there were no wires or leads connecting it to the interior of the bomb. He set the tape carefully aside and took a long look at the inside of the casing. The ticking was much louder now, and came from a rotary clockwork of some kind that was spinning ominously near the bottom edge of the device. There was a fairly sizable chunk of plastic explosive buried in its heart, connected with wires to the clockwork and also to what looked like pieces of a wireless phone. Bolan leaned in and smelled the explosive.

"Semtex," he whispered. Becker's eyes widened. The German knew the word.

Rieck started to say something and stopped, dumbfounded, when Bolan took his phone from his pocket. Snapping it open, he used the secure phone's camera feature to snap a picture of the interior of the bomb. He pressed the speed-dial key that would transmit the photo, scrambled, to the Farm. Then he paused, glaring at the spinning mechanism, hoping they would have enough time.

There was no telling just what Iron Thunder had thought to accomplish by rigging Becker and then leaving him. The cult didn't seem terribly concerned with efficiency. They were more into statements, into style over substance. It was that ragged edge that separated the Iron Thunder cultists from those professional soldiers who'd attacked Rieck and Bolan at the coffee shop.

There was, however, no time to ponder that mystery now. It occurred to the soldier, as he waited, listening to the doomsday numbers fall, that there might be a camera somewhere nearby. The Iron Thunder terrorists who'd done this to Becker could be watching to see the man blown up, savoring his last fear-filled moments on earth. If the bomb was capable of remote detonation, however, it stood to reason that anyone with a finger on that button would have pressed it as soon as Bolan started to tamper with it.

The secure phone began to vibrate, and Rieck nearly jumped out of his skin. Bolan glanced at him before keying the reply button. "Cooper," he said. Answering with his cover identity told anyone on the other end that he wasn't alone.

"Mr. Cooper," Aaron "the Bear" Kurtzman said, being cautious lest whomever was with Bolan could overhear, "I've just received your message. You'll be pleased to know that Mr. Akira has found corresponding schematics. I'm transferring you now."

"Understood," Bolan said quietly.

"Akira here," Akira Tokaido said. The young computer hacker was all-business now. He was particularly good with intricate electronic devices, which was likely why Kurtzman had tasked him with this problem. "It is a fairly conventional device," Akira reported. "Our recognition programs have identified all of the visible components as COTS," he continued, "commercial and off-the-shelf. That block of plastic explosive, is it C-4?"

"Semtex, by the odor," Bolan corrected.

"Ah, the color of the photo is a little washed out. No matter. You are ready?"

"Hurry," Bolan said.

"The two cards connected to the small transmitter on the right-hand side," Tokaido stated. "Those are from a cell phone. They can be removed without detonating the device. Simply pull them out and yank the wires free."

Bolan gritted his teeth, reached out and pulled the components free. Becker shut his eyes tightly. No explosion came.

"Still here," Bolan said softly.

"Now, the timer circuit," Tokaido said. "This is more complicated. There should be a third wire, not visible to me, somewhere near the two that are visible at the base of the rotary timer. You will have to find that third wire and cut it. Cut *only* the third wire."

Bolan set the phone on the floor and used the tip of his knife as a probe, careful not to slice into the insulation covering the two wires that had been visible in the photograph. He eased these aside, prying them gently, careful not to separate them. Beneath these black wires he found a third, blue wire, well hidden and also connected to the timing mechanism.

"I have a blue wire," he said, picking up the phone.

"The color is not important," Tokaido said. "The third wire is the detonation one. Cutting it alone deactivates the timer. Sever either of the other two wires and the circuit closes, detonating the bomb."

"Copy that," Bolan said. Once more setting down the phone, he put his fingers to his lips and then placed his hand on Becker's shoulder. He pointed at the bomb and then gestured with the dagger. The meaning was clear enough. Becker closed his eyes again and did his best to stay very still.

The timing cylinder began to spin more quickly.

"Great," Bolan muttered.

Rieck, looking over his shoulder, gasped. Like Bolan, he could understand what that meant: the timer had run down and the mechanism was going to trigger the explosive.

Bolan cut the wire. All three men held their breath.

There was a loud metallic *ping* as the mechanical trigger closed.

"Well," Bolan said. "That's that." He cut the straps holding the bomb to Becker's chest, removed the device and set it next to the chair.

Becker breathed hard, muttering "thank you" in German over and over again.

"Now what?" Rieck asked. He stepped to the nearest window and glanced out, checking the street beyond.

"Now we keep moving," Bolan said. "Obviously, Iron Thunder has been and gone. We need to follow the next lead in the chain. That means—"

"Cooper," Rieck interrupted. "Trouble."

"How many?" Bolan asked, checking his Beretta.

"Two more cars full of our well-armed, well-dressed friends."

"This is starting to get repetitive," Bolan said, nodding to Becker. "Explain to him what's going on." He looked around, noted the incongruously large bathroom off this room, which was apparently Becker's study. "Tell him to get into the bathtub and keep his head down. Tell him to stay down until the shooting stops. Stay here and shoot anyone who comes through that door that isn't me."

"And you?"

"I'm taking the fight to them." He secured the Beretta 93-R with a full 20-round magazine, then drew the Desert Eagle and checked it. A .44 Magnum round waited in the chamber and the magazine was topped off.

"I don't blame you," Rieck said.

"What?"

"Well, after all that trouble we took to save him," Rieck said with a grin, "I'll be damned if it's fair to have the second string take him out."

Bolan offered him a vertical salute with the barrel of the Desert Eagle. He let the weapon lead him as he walked out into the scorched corridor beyond.

5

The professional shooters were, much to Bolan's complete lack of surprise, armed with Heckler & Koch submachine guns. These were UMPs, in .40 or .45 caliber from the look of them. The men were exiting their Mercedes sedans as the Executioner came out to meet them. He strode out the front door of the building as the two teams converged on it.

"Guten tag." Bolan greeted them in his limited German, smiling broadly.

The two men in the lead stopped short and exchanged glances, confused by his sudden appearance and friendly demeanor.

The Desert Eagle whipped up from behind Bolan's back. The soldier aimed by instinct and shot the first man in the face, riding out the .44 Magnum recoil and bringing the barrel back on target. The second .44 slug cracked like thunder and blew the second man to the ground. The blitz had the desired effect. The shooters scattered, their initiative lost, as Bolan dropped two more of the retreating gunmen with expertly placed Magnum bullets.

Bolan ducked back inside the building, changing magazines on the run.

He counted the numbers in his head. A few seconds to take cover. A couple more to regroup and realize the gunfire had stopped. Then two more as they formed up and took the doorway....

The soldier broke left at the first corner, then pressed himself against the wall. As he figured they would, the gunmen hosed the hallway. The holes they left in the facing wall were large enough to be .45. Bolan had seen enough in his War Everlasting to be able to gauge them by eye.

There was a pause as the first shooters ran dry, but Bolan waited. A second volley sounded as the men behind the first gunners opened up. They were good at what they did, he had to admit. After the way he'd taken away their momentum, they were doing everything possible to grab it back, and taking no chances besides.

Footfalls rang on the hardwood floor of the corridor as the gunmen filed in. As experienced operatives they would take the corner wide, looking for someone hiding just as Bolan was doing. It was what the big American would have done if their roles were reversed. He let them get roughly halfway down the hall. Then he drew the Beretta 93-R left-handed and, with a gun in each fist, threw himself to the floor.

The shooters caught the movement and triggered withering blasts from their UMPs, but Bolan was at least two feet below their line of fire. As he hit the ground, ignoring the jolt in his shoulder and left arm, he started to shoot. The Desert Eagle boomed in his right hand as 3-round bursts of 9 mm fury tore the air from his left. He was careful to take at least one man in the knees, folding him over, while drilling the other gunners with head shots and center-of-mass groupings.

Empty shells were still clattering on the hardwood floor as the last of the gunmen went sprawling.

Bolan rolled and surged to his feet, closing in on the man he'd wounded. He planted a knee in the gunman's chest and kicked the UMP aside, the barrel of his Desert Eagle pressed into his captive's throat. Through the pain from his shattered kneecaps, the man looked up at him with undisguised contempt.

"English," Bolan said. "Do you speak it?"

"Ja," the man grunted.

"Who do you work for?"

"I am unemployed." The gunner's accent was heavy, but not indecipherable.

Bolan pressed harder with the Desert Eagle. "I don't have time to argue. There's a lot of work to do. If you won't tell me what I need to know, you're useless to me. And I don't intend to spend any time looking over my shoulder." It was all for the gunman's benefit, of course; if he couldn't provide any useful information, Bolan would write him off and have Rieck contact the appropriate authorities to have the man processed by the locals. There was no way the gunman could know that, however. He had just watched Bolan shoot down more than half-a-dozen other men.

"I cannot tell you," the man said. "I would forfeit too much. I cannot. Please. Do not force me."

"If you're worried about family, or your own life," Bolan offered, "we can protect you. Tell me what you know."

"I cannot—" The man stopped talking. He was looking at something behind Bolan, something that the soldier could hear, too. The sound of something heavy and metallic rolling on the hardwood floor.

The grenade came to a stop three feet away, resting against the sole of a dead gunner's shoe.

Bolan acted on pure reflex. He dived over top the wounded gunner and just made the protection of the hall corner. The explosion was deafening, like a hammer blow, vibrating through his head and washing over his frame. The world faded to gray around the edges, threatening to go black. He clenched his fists, the pistols in his hands anchoring him to the land of the living as the blast faded.

Rieck emerged from the stairwell opposite. Bolan waved him off, the ringing in his ears still almost too much for conscious thought. The agent was saying something. Bolan shook his head and pointed to the exit around the corner.

"Okay?" Rieck was asking.

"What?" Bolan asked. He realized he could hear his own voice and the Interpol agent's, too.

"Are you all right?" the man shouted.

"I'm fine," Bolan said. "Come on!" He ran for it. Rieck followed.

They hit the street at a dead run. Bolan radically altered his course as he left the building, hoping to throw off any sniper who might be lying in wait. No shots came. He paused, crouching behind one of the Mercedes. The door to the vehicle was open and the keys were in it. The previous passengers wouldn't be needing the car anytime soon.

"Cooper!" Rieck shouted, gesturing. Bolan heard the little Vespa scooter as Rieck pointed it out to him. The rider, indistinct in a hooded sweatshirt, glanced their way before hunkering down over the handlebars. The scooter shot into an alleyway between two nearby buildings.

"Come on," Bolan said again. He jumped into the Mercedes. Rieck took the passenger side, the shotgun awkward as he folded himself into the vehicle. They paralleled the scooter's course. The driver of the Vespa wasn't stupid. The scooter couldn't outrun the Mercedes, but it could go where the large car couldn't. Bolan kept the pedal down as far as he dared, navigating the narrow streets, keeping the scooter in sight as he tracked its movements.

"Who are we chasing?" Rieck asked.

Bolan shook his head, still shrugging off the effects of the explosion. "Grenade thrower."

"How do you know this is your guy?" Rieck pointed at the Vespa, visible for a moment through a gap between buildings.

"Timing is everything," Bolan said. He stayed on the motor-scooter's tail, whipping the responsive Mercedes through turn after turn, reducing the distance between the two vehicles.

"There!" Rieck pointed again. The street forked, and the right-hand branch intercepted the parallel street on which the scooter now traveled. Bolan, grateful for the light traffic at that late hour, urged more speed from the engine. The Mercedes growled and surged forward.

The Vespa's driver saw the threat too late.

Metal screamed as the big automobile plowed into the small vehicle. The hooded driver hit the car's windshield with enough force to crack it, bouncing and rolling off onto the pavement. Bolan brought the Mercedes to a halt, whipping the wheel sideways to avoid crushing his quarry. Then he was up and out, the Beretta 93-R trained on the prone form.

"Hands!" he ordered. "Show me your hands!" Behind him, Rieck translated into German, managing to sound as forceful as the soldier. The hooded figure remained immobile.

"Rieck," Bolan said, never taking his eyes off the prone form. "Cover me. Could be shamming."

"Understood," Rieck said. He held his shotgun at the ready.

Bolan moved in, careful in his positioning. He put a booted toe in the body's flank and pushed. The hood came free, and a young man stared upward, blinking. He groaned.

"Don't move," Bolan instructed firmly. Rieck translated again.

"Do not…do not shoot," the man said, in English. "I will not resist."

"Are you armed?"

"I have two more grenades," the young man admitted. "In the pocket, here." He indicated the center pouch of the hooded sweatshirt. "I will not reach for them."

Bolan dragged the man up and propped him against the Mercedes, hands on its hood. He searched him thoroughly, finding the grenades. These were old, possibly World War II vintage.

"Are those…?" Rieck asked.

"American, originally." Bolan nodded. "There's no way to know how long they've been kicking around the black market arms channels."

"He's awfully cooperative for a death cultist," Rieck said.

Bolan, satisfied the man had nothing else on him, turned him over and pointed the barrel of the 93-R at his face.

"I...please do not kill me," the man said. "Yes, I am Iron Thunder."

"Three seconds," Bolan said simply. "Tell us everything you know. Why did you attack me? What was your purpose here? And how did you find us?"

"You misunderstand," the man said. "I..." He paused, his face turning red. He began to sag against the car. Bolan, alarmed, eased him to the ground. The sudden loss of tension in his muscles was so total it was hard to believe it could be faked.

"Cooper?" Rieck asked. "What's happening to him?"

"Poison," Bolan said grimly.

"Yes," the man said. "I simply...I did not wish to be shot. Guns are so ugly. My mother...she will want to pay her... her..." He stopped then. Bolan watched the light leave the young man's eyes.

"How did he do it?" Rieck asked, moving to stand over the body with Bolan.

"It wasn't very fast acting," he said. "He might even have taken it before he started running. There's no way to know. And there's no telling just how fanatical he might have been, how dedicated to Iron Thunder's message. Or they could be more rational than we think, and he took something, a pill or capsule of some kind, after he hit the pavement."

"More rational than we think?" Rieck shook his head. "After those two women, I can't say I have much hope of that."

"Me, neither."

"I'd better get on it," Rieck said, taking his phone from his coat. "I'm not sure why all this hasn't drawn the police before now. Something strange is going on."

Bolan left Rieck to wait with the body of the scooter jockey while he drove back to Becker's condominium building. The local police were starting to arrive and set up as he got there. It was too soon for Rieck's call to have made a difference, so someone had to have put in a call.

The soldier stopped and conferred with the officer in charge of the scene, who spoke English haltingly but made his displeasure with the situation abundantly clear. Bolan apologized, in his limited German, for being unable to communicate better. Then he retreated to the Mercedes to await Rieck's return. The locals were searching the corpses and assessing the crime scene, and Bolan could only hope they did their jobs reasonably well. It would not do to butt heads with them directly until Rieck was back here to lend him credibility with the police.

He checked in with the Farm. A worried Barbara Price, Stony Man's mission controller, sounded relieved when he explained the bomb had been successfully defused. Bolan updated her on his progress—their on-again, off-again relationship was something neither of them let get in the way of the Farm's business—and got the latest situation updates, which Price transmitted directly to Bolan's secure phone.

"All right, Barb," he said finally, watching another marked police car pull up. Rieck exited the passenger side. He was talking animatedly into his phone, hopefully running interference with the locals. Bolan knew only too well how the lords of these little bureaucratic fiefdoms tended to react when he marched through their territory, slashing and burning in pursuit of a mission. No doubt to those accustomed to a reasonably quiet watch, the city was in the grip of all-out war by comparison. No, scratch that, he thought; it wasn't "by comparison" at all. This was war, it had always been war, and it was the same war he'd waged for years.

Rieck was now pacing back and forth alongside the Mercedes. Bolan, never one to remain idle, busied himself with searching the car. He found a spare set of keys, a magazine for a Heckler & Koch USP pistol, and a small sheaf of rumpled road maps. Beneath these, however, was something else.

He turned the item over in his fingers. It was a magnetic key card, bearing a company logo that meant nothing to him. There were no words, no numbers and no other lettering of any kind. It wasn't a credit card. It resembled the computerized key cards used by hotels.

Rieck ended his call and leaned into the open doorway of the driver's side. "What's that?" he asked, pointing.

"Just possibly," Bolan said, "a break." He handed the card to Rieck. "Can you get this couriered through channels, fast?"

"Sure," Rieck said. "Just give me an address."

Bolan rattled it off from memory. The place was one of the local safehouses and drop points arranged for his visit to Germany. Anything sent there would find its way to the Farm or, more likely, a local lab on whose personnel Brognola could count for cooperation, maybe CIA or a related and reliable foreign agency. If there was anything to be found, the data would be relayed to the Farm for analysis, and Kurtzman and his people would make sure the Executioner knew about it.

"All right," Bolan said. "Now we wait."

"You don't want to move on the next target?" Rieck asked.

"After this firestorm?" Bolan jerked his chin toward the building. Becker, with a blanket over his shoulders, was being led out the front under heavy guard. The local equivalent of SWAT, heavily armed and wearing goggles, helmets and ballistic vests, formed a cordon around him and walked him to one of the waiting ambulances. No doubt he would get a police escort to the hospital, where he could be treated. Then he would most likely end up at a safehouse. Bolan wondered just what the locals thought they would do beyond that.

"You think they'll clear out any of Becker's assets," Rieck guessed.

"Or be waiting for us." Bolan nodded. "Either way, I think we've dragged our feet through enough trip wires for one day. Go home, Rieck. Get some sleep. If tonight is any indication, you're going to need it."

6

David Schucker watched the dawn.

From the window of his office in the Security Consortium's state-of-the-art Berlin headquarters, the company's head of operations watched the gray rays of the day's first light touch each building in turn. This was Schucker's favorite part of the day. The city, indeed the world, was so full of endless possibility with each new dawn.

The soft knock on the heavy, polished wooden door made him frown.

It would be Gunnar, of course. Only Gunnar insisted on knocking rather than using the intercom. No matter how many times Schucker told him to do so, Gunnar insisted on rapping lightly on the door itself. Schucker had finally given up, resigned to this tiny irritant. The problem was that Gunnar's visits never *remained* tiny irritants. The field commander for Schucker's security operatives never bothered Schucker in person unless he was summoned, or unless he had bad news.

"Enter," Schucker said reluctantly. Gunnar Heinriksen looked almost sheepish as he walked into the luxuriously appointed office, closing the door quietly behind him. He moved to stand at attention in front of Schucker's desk, his eyes forward and seemingly staring blankly out the window.

This was bad; Schucker knew Gunnar refused to make eye contact only when he felt his employer would be especially outraged.

Schucker sighed. "Very well, Gunnar," he said in German. "Tell me."

"Sir." Heinriksen snapped his heels together. He was a very large man, broad through the shoulders and as solid as a boulder. He never looked very comfortable in the dark suits he wore, as if the seams of the expensive custom garments might split at any moment. The bulge of the ridiculously large pistol he wore in a shoulder holster was visible under his blazer. The early-morning sunlight reflected from his shaved, bullet-shaped skull, while the craggy face beneath the bald pate was creased with worry.

"Out with it, Gunnar," Schucker growled. "I'm in no mood."

"We've lost the teams, sir," Heinriksen stated.

"Which teams?" Schucker demanded.

"All. All of them, sir. Each team from yesterday…gone."

Schucker blinked. "What do you mean, gone?"

"Down, sir," Heinriksen said. "Shot."

"That's ridiculous," Schucker spit. "Dumar's people don't have the skill or even the weapons to stand against us, and they've no reason yet to suspect—"

"Uh, no, sir," Heinriksen said, so flustered he actually interrupted Schucker in midsentence. "Dumar's people are not involved, sir. It was the Interpol agent, and someone with him."

Schucker stood up, his fingertips brushing his gleaming glass-and-metal desk. "Gunnar," he said quietly, "if you don't start making sense I shall quite possibly have you shot."

"Sir—" Heinriksen shook his head, as if trying to ward off Schucker's anger through denial "—per your instructions, I had several security teams shadowing Dumar's field people."

Schucker snorted. "Field people" to Dumar simply meant whomever he could find who didn't mind pulling a trigger, no matter how sloppy the jobs that got done. They were bloodthirsty, yes, and fierce, but all of Dumar Eon's most capable killers were amateurs, little better than dangerous wild animals. Calling them "field people" galled Schucker, but he knew better than to argue the point. Gunnar could be quite defensive when pressed, and there was no need to sidetrack him further. The big man paused, trying to gather his thoughts.

"Yes, Gunnar, I know," Schucker prodded. "Continue."

"Sir, we tracked the group sent to assassinate the Interpol agent assigned to the case, the man named Rieck. He met with someone, an American, apparently. Our source does not know for which agency this man works. Our team was not in time to prevent the attempted assassination."

"I feared as much," Schucker said. "They lack skill, but have no shortage of desire. Such murderers are hard to stop. It was precisely such a mess I had hoped to prevent or, failing that, wipe out utterly. That idiot Dumar! Killing an Interpol agent is sure to raise suspicions. It runs a very real risk of exposing our operations. So? What happened?"

"The two of them, the Interpol agent and the American, defeated Dumar's assassins."

"Which is also not that great a surprise," Schucker said. "I left orders that if Dumar's people failed, of which there was considerable chance, they were to be eliminated to prevent any liabilities, any possible tracing back to the Consortium. And that any and all witnesses be removed."

"Yes, sir, I know, sir." Heinriksen nodded. "They did not have the opportunity. The team was taken out. All of them, sir. Shot by Rieck and the American."

"You're kidding," Schucker said, his jaw dropping. "By two men?"

"No, sir. I mean, yes, sir."

"What of the security team assigned to purge Becker's home?"

"Also dead, sir," Heinriksen said hurriedly. "We were too late to stop Dumar's people from making the first move on Becker in his home. As you suspected, it looks as though they left considerable evidence behind. I have seen the reports, copied by our paid informants in the police. Dumar's people left Becker alive, strapped to a bomb, in order to make one of their…statements."

"Fools," Schucker muttered. "I *knew* they were planning to do something stupid."

"Yes, sir. And as you ordered, the men detailed to Becker's home knew they were to make sure of his death and burn his home to the ground, to erase any trace of Dumar's activities."

"And?"

"Rieck and the American again, sir." Heinriksen frowned deeply, further creasing his pocked face. "None of the operatives escaped. My sources within the police say it was a slaughter."

"I don't believe it," Schucker said. He sat down heavily. After taking a few breaths, he tightened his jaw and looked at Heinriksen sharply. "You have the men you need for the exchange?"

"Yes, sir. The materials were relocated early this morning. We will have everything ready when Bashir and his people arrive."

"Dumar has no reason to suspect?"

"I do not believe so, sir," Heinriksen said. "And he has no immediate plans for the materials of which we are aware. Depending on how vigilant he is, however, he will know eventually. We left little behind."

"That I have planned for," Schucker said. "But losing so many operatives and failing to eliminate so many liabilities… *this* I did not anticipate. Gunnar, the situation is delicate."

"Yes, sir."

"You know what must be done to prepare for the meeting with Bashir," Schucker said. "See to it. No mistakes."

"Yes, sir,"

"Have Dumar's plans for today changed?"

"No, sir. Our spies within Iron Thunder say the rally is still on for today. Dumar has given no indication of what his address is to involve, or at least, none our people could discover. But he will be occupied with the rally for some time, which will prevent him and most of Iron Thunder from focusing on other issues."

"Good. Now go. We'll have to determine how best to deal with this Interpol investigation, but it will take planning."

Heinriksen snapped his heels again. He spun on one leg and disappeared as quietly as he had arrived, easing the door shut behind him.

Schucker let out an exasperated breath. Finally, he swiveled in his high-backed leather chair to gaze once more out the window. The sun was now fully visible, bathing the buildings below and throwing broad shadows across the streets.

Damn that Dumar!

Schucker stood again and began pacing. It would be necessary to form contingency plans, and to draft more manpower from other Consortium operations throughout Germany. He would also need to perform a great deal of damage control, and throw around a great deal of money. The security personnel would be identified, and their employment to the Consortium was traceable. Plausible deniability might be found in one or two cases, perhaps half a dozen, but so many dead bodies above and beyond that would raise too many questions.

He began to tick off his mental list of police and government officials, men and women known to be receptive to bribes. It would be expensive, but as long as he kept them fat and happy, the public officials on his payroll would find some excuse in each case. They would shelve any ongoing investigations and dismiss the deaths with something the news media could repeat with breathless credulity. Perhaps a drug war. Yes, that would be simple enough. Drug wars were always popular. The drugs involved didn't even matter, really. People were always willing to believe that purveyors of unnamed drugs were always shooting one another over deals gone bad. It didn't matter that such behavior was no way to conduct business, and flew in the face of the best interests of all involved. The public would believe it, and that was all that mattered to the politicians and the police. With their consciences clean, their records intact and their wallets full, they would dance to whatever tune Schucker played for them.

The Interpol investigation upset him very much. Now, especially now, with the Syrians on their way and the first of many profitable deals about to be brokered, the Consortium couldn't afford official scrutiny. Had Dumar Eon not behaved so rashly, Schucker could have kept the investigators busy for weeks. He could have kept them trapped in a morass of red tape and false leads, thinking they were accomplishing something, while the Consortium went about its business unmolested. But no, as soon as Eon learned of this Rieck's identity, he'd had the man followed, and fully intended to kill him. In a public place, no less! Eon and his stupid statements, Schucker thought. He wouldn't be satisfied until the entire world collapsed around his head and took him with it. And of course, that was the problem.

Schucker had been Eon's most trusted operative within the Consortium since its inception. The Leader of Iron Thunder trusted him to run the day-to-day operations of the company, to take care of the details, to keep the money flowing, and to see to the fine points of the Consortium's various acquisitions. That was why the security personnel on whom Schucker relied—mercenaries, former military men, a few former government agents and other trained soldiers—had been cultivated, their ranks expanded over the years to form a private army of sorts. Yes, they made it possible for the Consortium to do what it did, as had Iron Thunder's cultists. Both were "muscle" in the most primitive sense, and both had helped, at various times and to varying degrees of subtlety—or its lack—to clear the way for important Consortium acquisitions. But Iron Thunder's aberrant mental cases were most certainly not the professionals Schucker had hired. He'd seen to their training, organized them and put them in place where they afforded him the most strategic value. They were the mechanism whereby he would free the Consortium of Eon's poisonous and unstable influence. The Consortium's security personnel were Schucker's men, and they answered to him alone. They were *not* Eon's cultists. The difference was like night and day.

The company had grown beyond the man calling himself "Dumar Eon." Schucker thought this had been a long time coming, and in truth, had he been as confident a year ago as he was now, he'd have made his move then. The change was long overdue. The Consortium was a business, had become a business precisely because Schucker, hired and left to run its operations by Eon, had proved more than equal to the task. Eon didn't appreciate what the Consortium could be, or didn't care. No, in his mind, everything came down to that bizarre near-religion of his, and damn the consequences.

Eon wasn't stupid; Schucker knew that only too well. But he *was* overconfident. He believed Schucker and the other high-level members of the Consortium's management were pawns, tools who were willing to see to the company's expansion and funnel the profits to Iron Thunder as long as their own pockets were well lined.

It hadn't taken long for Schucker to realize just how insane Eon was. He had lived with that knowledge for some time. For the most part, it hadn't mattered—except Eon was becoming increasingly haphazard, his people increasingly sloppy and reckless in their methods. The cult's beliefs were becoming more and more immediate to Dumar, who until recently had seemed content to watch the operation grow, and to keep his followers busy with his various electronic pronouncements and inspirational speeches. It was, Schucker knew, only a matter of time before Eon managed to crash the entire company. He would probably stage some major spectacle for Iron Thunder's benefit, and quite possibly get himself killed along the way.

Schucker couldn't allow that.

There was tremendous potential for profit within the Consortium, provided it was run carefully. Eon had his own reasons for the accomplishments the company had seen to date, and until recently those had coincided with Schucker's ambitions. At least, they hadn't interfered with his ambitions. But Schucker was a forward-thinking man, and he had foreseen this day, had anticipated the point at which Eon's devotion to his sad death cult and Schucker's desire to maintain the Consortium's profitability would become increasingly opposed. It was entirely possible that Eon didn't see it that way, at least not yet. This was irrelevant. Schucker knew the situation was untenable, would be irreparable in a few more years or even less. Thus, some six months ago, he had finally begun taking concrete, irreversible steps. He had crossed the point of no return. He had implemented a plan the wheels of which, once turning, couldn't be stopped without exposing himself and his people to Eon's wrath.

So be it.

It had been easy to assign his security personnel to follow Eon's people. The cultists were in no way professionals and had no reason to believe they were suspect. It had, similarly, been easy enough to infiltrate Iron Thunder itself. Eon had released enough videos that any reasonably flexible operatives could memorize and parrot these back to him, playing the roles of true believers, who were welcomed into the Iron Thunder fold. It was from these men and women that Schucker always learned of Eon's plans…eventually.

That was the frustrating part. Eon was a fairly insular man, for all his charisma, and word of his plans took time to trickle down to the lesser members of Iron Thunder. Trickle down it *did*, for Eon wasn't nearly as adept at keeping secrets as he liked to believe. But the time involved meant that Schucker was always a step behind Eon, always playing cleanup and catch-up, always mopping up the crazed cult leader's messes. The potential disasters that Schucker and his personnel were required to cover up were becoming more and more difficult to hide, as evidenced by this latest set of massacres. The thought galled Schucker intensely.

David Schucker knew that he was the future of the Consortium. Eon wanted to stage some fantastic *götterdämmerung*, some spectacular destructive culmination of his cult's work. He wasn't so secretive in his desires that Schucker didn't know that. The conflagration Eon envisioned would of course consume the Consortium and all those associated with it. Schucker was careful not to reveal that to other executives within the Consortium, for it wouldn't pay to make them nervous. He had enough to deal with.

He had been planning his takeover of the Consortium almost since his first days with it. He had hoped to maneuver Eon and Iron Thunder out of the picture quietly and gradually. It might still be possible, though he would have to examine his timetable and see to the forcible removal of some of the more rogue elements among the cultists. And that would eventually include their leader. Schucker could see to that. And once it was done, he could continue providing weapons to the West's enemies at considerable financial gain to himself and the Consortium's stakeholders.

He had no illusions. He knew full well that many would suffer because of what he would broker to the world's terrorist states. He saw it as only just. Born of German Jews, Schucker lived with the knowledge that both his parents had died at the hands of a government the hypocritical West had refused to stop until it was too late. It mattered little to Schucker what had happened subsequently, or how the war had ended. He knew only that he had grown up an orphan because those in power had not cared to intervene until their own interests were endangered. This was a powerful lesson for him, perhaps the first he remembered internalizing. It, as much as anything, was his religion, his philosophy. Schucker intended to become wealthier each day. He would do so knowing that men, women and children suffered and died at the hands of those he empowered.

And he didn't care.

The world was a cruel place. Schucker lived with that knowledge. It was a dull ache in the back of his brain, always. He saw no reason, therefore, not to enrich himself by trading on that truth. What was truth, after all, but an asset, a commodity? He who was aware of it could use it to his own ends, and to hell with anyone who got in the way.

Schucker frowned. There was much work to be done. It wasn't personal. It was never personal. It was always business.

But a few people would have to die, anyway.

7

"Nice ride," Rieck commented when he observed Bolan's silver-gray BMW 7 series sedan. He stepped from the curb in front of his hotel, where, by phone, Bolan had requested they meet that morning. Both men had taken the opportunity to grab a few hours of sleep. Now it was time to follow the next thread in this doomsday patchwork.

"It's a rental," Bolan said.

"*Mine* is a rental." He climbed into the passenger seat.

"Well, so is mine," Bolan said simply.

"You have friends in high places."

Bolan said nothing.

They pulled away from the curb, the BMW accelerating smoothly. A throaty rumble hummed from deep within its power plant. Rieck took the opportunity to remove the Heckler & Koch MP-5 K from under his trench coat, checking it to verify that the magazine was full but there was no round in the chamber. Bolan raised an eyebrow.

"There was a lot of paperwork to fill out," Rieck said sheepishly.

"Feeling outgunned?" Bolan asked.

"Not anymore." Rieck grinned. Bolan allowed himself a smile at that.

They drove across town, Bolan making his way through the traffic with little difficulty. While Berlin wasn't one of his usual haunts, the Executioner had visited the city enough times to know its layout.

"I confirmed the address you gave me this morning," Rieck said, returning the MP-5 K to the folds of his coat. He had it riding in a shoulder strap. It was a common enough method for toting the tiny submachine gun. The weapon, while small for its type, was still quite bulky for on-body concealment purposes.

"You did it yourself?" Bolan asked.

"Yes." Rieck nodded. "I made sure no one saw me access the computer. If we have a leak, I didn't want to take any chances. Whoever put those killers on my trail doesn't need to know what we're up to this morning. Uh, by the way, Cooper, what *are* we up to this morning?"

"That magnetic key card I had you process through channels," Bolan said, "is from a secure storage area."

"Yes, that much I confirmed," Rieck stated. "It's an industrial locker, the sort of place construction companies and chemical houses store items they don't want to leave lying around."

"Which begs the question," Bolan said. "Why was a professional shooter, presumably trying to murder Becker on the heels of the terrorist assault on his home, carrying this card? That's what I intend to find out." He produced the card from a pocket of the combat blacksuit he wore under his drover coat. "It was couriered back to me early this morning. The storage locker is unit 226."

"What do you expect to find?"

"If I knew that, we wouldn't need to check it," Bolan said. "We need more intel. Following a priority list of likely targets isn't going to put us ahead of Iron Thunder. It'll leave us a step behind in every case. We need some insight, something that can give us an inside track."

"Fair enough."

They found the storage facility without incident. There were no guards. The lockers were grouped in neat rows, with alleyways in between. Bolan drove directly to unit 226. If the door spacing was any indication, this was a very large enclosure, though from the outside it was no different from any of the other units. Bolan guided the vehicle in a circle around the storage unit, checking the adjacent alleyways, making sure there were no nasty surprises. Then he parked, slinging his canvas war bag over his shoulder as he climbed out. His drover coat covered his other weapons. The bag, on its broad shoulder strap, contained a variety of little surprises courtesy of Stony Man Farm's armorer, John "Cowboy" Kissinger.

Rieck stood guard as Bolan swiped the key card in the electronic lock. When the LEDs on the lock began to flash green, he raised the overhead door, one hand on the butt of his Beretta 93-R.

"Well," Rieck said.

"Yeah." Bolan nodded.

The storage locker was empty. Bolan eyed the space warily. He took his CombatLight from its position clipped to his pocket and played the powerful beam around the empty unit.

"Making sure?" Rieck asked.

"Checking for booby traps," Bolan said. "Lasers, trip wires, that sort of thing." Rieck paled a bit at that.

Bolan shrugged, put the light away and walked into the storage locker. He checked each wall by feel. Rieck glanced inside, looked up and paused.

"Hey, Cooper," he said, pointing. "Up there."

Bolan followed his gesture and found the small slip of paper, where it had become lodged in the metal accordion folds of the roll-up security door. He reached up and plucked it free. It was handwritten in German, in cramped script, but appeared to be a bulleted list. He handed the paper to Rieck.

The Interpol agent scanned the list. "Cooper, if I'm not wrong, this is a manifest. This last item?" He pointed to one of the bullets. "That's a nerve agent."

Bolan frowned, then he reached for his secure satellite phone. "Repeat that for me, so I get the pronunciation just right," he began. "If we can—"

The sound of engines interrupted him. Sliding van doors were opening, and there were shouts of alarm.

"Oh, shit," Rieck said.

Bolan drew the Beretta. He peered out from behind the door opening, careful to expose only one eye.

Three cargo vans had parked behind and next to the BMW, blocking it in. Men and women, all of them relatively young and dressed in street clothes, were climbing out, pointing and shouting in German.

"'The stuff, the stuff,'" Rieck translated. "'It is gone. They have taken it.'"

Bolan raised an eyebrow. The nearest man suddenly shouted, *"Eisen-Donner! Eisen-Donner!"* Bolan knew that tone. It was a battle cry.

"Iron Thunder," Rieck said unnecessarily.

Bolan flicked the Beretta's fire selector switch to 3-round burst. Rieck pulled the MP-5 K to full extension on its shoulder sling, slapping the charging handle to chamber the first round.

The Iron Thunder cultists cut loose.

Bolan and Rieck ducked back to either side of the open doorway. The metal storage building wasn't up to the onslaught; rays of sunlight punched through behind a hail of bullets from the cultists' weapons. Both men hit the ground, and bullets tore the air above them as the Iron Thunder gunners opened up at waist level, hosing the storage locker without much thought to targeting. There was no subtlety in the attack, and no attempt to conceal their actions. There was only viciousness and brutality.

This, Bolan could deal with.

The soldier reached into his war bag with his left hand, producing a small fragmentation grenade. He popped the pin with his thumb, let the spoon spring free, and rolled the small bomb through the open doorway.

"Brace yourself!" he told Rieck.

The explosion reverberated through the storage unit, beating it like a steel drum. The closest of the vans was slapped aside a few feet, bouncing on its springs. The Iron Thunder shooters scattered. The initiative was now Bolan's. He gestured to Rieck, drew the Desert Eagle with his left hand and charged forward with both guns leading.

The first of the cultists was caught flat-footed. Bolan's 9 mm burst punched him in the chest and left him upright against one of the cargo vans, a look of numb shock on his face. He folded. Bolan skirted the vehicle, both guns shooting flame. The suppressed coughs of the Beretta contrasted with the booming thunder of the Desert Eagle, but both weapons dealt deadly justice as the Executioner worked his way through the disorganized cult members.

Rieck took the opposite side of the van Bolan had approached, his MP-5 K gripped firmly in his hands. Bolan caught him in his peripheral vision, again applying his textbook submachine-gun stance, pumping out perfectly timed bursts into the running Iron Thunder gunners. A few shots were starting to peg the asphalt near the Interpol agent's feet, but he ignored them. The enemy didn't yet have his range, and he seemed to know it.

Bolan put thoughts of his ally out of his mind, confident that Rieck could take care of himself. A cultist broke cover in front of them, rolling out of an alleyway between two storage buildings. He managed to off a shot from the large revolver he wielded before Bolan put a .44 slug through his head. The body crumpled, dead long before it stopped falling.

The cultists who remained—armed with a motley collection of handguns, sawed-off shotguns and a couple of cutdown rifles—broke and ran. Rieck shouted something that Bolan couldn't hear, but the meaning was clear enough: he was pursuing. The big American tracked his own targets and went after the group running opposite to Rieck's. A third knot of cultists were fleeing through the storage complex alleys in yet another direction, but there was no way to get them all. Bolan knew better than to waste time trying, focusing instead on attainable goals. As he ran, however, one of the stragglers in the third group moved into the open space between buildings, silhouetting himself. Bolan snapped off a right-angle shot from the Desert Eagle as he raced after the other cultists. He didn't break stride to watch the body fall, a .44 Magnum hole between the dead cultist's shoulder blades.

The soldier was tracking a total of three Iron Thunder members—two young men and one woman. The trailing cultist, a man, triggered a shotgun blast at Bolan, losing his balance as he did so. The Executioner snapped a single shot from the Beretta into the faltering man's head, then vaulted the dead man and kept running, never slowing his pace.

The woman began to yell in German to the man just ahead of her. Her words had an effect; both cultists suddenly dropped their guns and jogged to a standstill. They put their hands in the air and turned slowly to face their pursuer. Bolan slowed, checking left and right in the alleyway, scanning the metal rooflines of the storage units. If this was a trick or some other kind of trap, he couldn't see it.

The woman began to speak in German, between great, racking inhalations as she tried to catch her breath. The man wasn't much better off. They were a nondescript pair, both blond, wearing college sweatshirts and stained, ripped blue jeans. The woman started to drop her hands, and Bolan extended the Desert Eagle toward her.

"Don't," he said simply.

"Bitte," the woman rasped, still breathing heavily.

"English," Bolan said. "If you have something to say, do it fast."

"Please—" she glanced at her counterpart and then back to the soldier "—we...we will not resist."

"If you move, you die," Bolan said. Even as he warned them, he was unsure how much good it would do. The group's sole purpose seemed to *be* for its members to die, preferably after or as they took others with them.

Bolan flipped the Desert Eagle's safety and holstered the big pistol in its Kydex waistband holster, bringing the Beretta 93-R up to cover the two runners. He was fully prepared to put a 3-round burst in each of them if need be. It had become only too clear just how dangerously vicious these Iron Thunder people could be.

"Lie down," he said, gesturing with his chin to the pavement. "Hands behind your heads, fingers laced together. Slowly."

The two cultists complied. Only then did Bolan move closer, kicking their weapons farther away. He stood behind them, his Beretta at the ready. There was no point in trying to search them by himself. The chances that one or both would try something were too great, and he didn't intend to lose any more prisoners.

"Hey!" Rieck called from down the alleyway. Bolan silently gave him credit for not shouting the soldier's cover identity. While Rieck was probably aware it was likely not Bolan's real name, or that at the very least it was *possibly* a cover, he wasn't broadcasting it to whomever might be in earshot.

"Here," Bolan called back.

"Don't shoot," Rieck said. "I'm coming in."

Moments later, he appeared, with one hand on the MP-5 K under his shoulder. He was a little flushed but otherwise looked unharmed.

"You okay?" Bolan asked.

"A little winded," Rieck admitted. "It's been too long since I used to run track." He extended the MP-5 K to cover the prisoners, when he realized they were alive. "I see you caught two."

"You?" Bolan asked.

"No." Rieck shook his head. "I shot two. One got away. We lost a few others in between."

"Can't be helped," Bolan said.

"Where have you taken it?" demanded the young man on the pavement, speaking up in accented English.

"Taken who?" Rieck asked. Bolan looked at him, then back at the prisoner.

"Not who," the young man spit. Bolan watched him closely; he was working himself up to make a move.

"All right," Rieck said. "Taken what? We haven't taken anything."

"It was *ours*," the woman said. "You had no right!"

"What was yours?" Rieck asked. When there was no response, he repeated the query in German—or so Bolan assumed—and then asked a few follow-up questions. The two prisoners started answering, rapidly, the woman sobbing and the man barking his responses angrily. Twice Bolan caught the name "Dumar."

"This is very strange," Rieck said, glancing at Bolan, the barrel of his MP-5 K still angled at the two Iron Thunder members. "They seem to think we've stolen the contents of the storage unit. They're intentionally vague about the goods, but it seems like nerve agent or something worse is just the start. It might have been explosives, or a mixture, but it was obviously big and probably quite deadly. They keep saying they need it for 'the moment,' whatever that is, and they're upset that Dumar Eon will be very angry with them for failing. I believe they were sent to take the contents of the storage unit in the vans to some other location."

"What location?" Bolan asked. He waited as Rieck and the prisoners spoke back and forth rapidly. The woman was still in tears.

"They don't know," Rieck announced finally. "The location was either known to the drivers, who've been killed or run off, or was to be phoned in to them. Neither of our friends here is aware of it."

Bolan said nothing at first. Finally, he stepped forward and knelt, placing the barrel of the Beretta against the woman's head. He locked eyes with the male, his gaze hard.

"Make sure he understands that I want to know, and if he doesn't tell me, I'm going to kill her." Bolan, of course, would do nothing of the kind, but his enemies had no way to know that.

Rieck translated the man's reply. "He said go ahead," the Interpol agent said. "He says he does not know her well and would not care if he did. He says the 'final release' awaits them all, and he hopes we will kill him, too."

The words were tough, but Bolan could read the fear in the young man's eyes.

"He doesn't know," the soldier finally agreed. "I'll keep an eye on these two. You make the necessary calls. We'll get this cleaned up and move out."

"I'm becoming very popular around here." Rieck sighed as he flipped open his wireless phone. Then he paused and looked at Bolan. "Cooper, if the weapons in that locker have been stolen, who's got them?"

"When we figure that out," Bolan said, "we'll know whose door to kick in."

8

"Understood," Rieck said. He closed the phone and put it back in his jacket. The BMW hummed as Bolan guided it through the streets of Berlin. He looked over at Rieck expectantly. The German rattled off an address and gave him directions, explaining that the location was a small pub some distance away.

"What's there?"

"We have an agent in Iron Thunder," Rieck said proudly.

"I wasn't told," Bolan said.

"Neither was I," Rieck explained. "Deep cover. Need to know only. I guess someone finally decided that I needed to know, and now I am telling you." He shook his head. "I have no idea how long he has been with the group, but my superiors tell me he has information for us. It is too important to be trusted to electronic communications, the agent says, and so we have to meet him in person. The meet was his choice, as is the location."

"Do you trust this?" Bolan asked.

"Before I met you, I would have." Rieck laughed bitterly. "But no, I do not think it's a trap. At least, I hope not."

Bolan looked at him and then returned his eyes to the road.

It took them ten minutes to reach the location. Bolan parked the BMW and the two men got out.

"Will you know him when you see him?" Bolan asked.

"No," Rieck admitted. "But he knows me, apparently. He'll have to let us know when he sees me."

Bolan frowned. He didn't like this. His Beretta and Desert Eagle were reloaded and ready; he didn't need to check them. He opened his three-quarter-length drover coat a bit more to allow for a smooth, uninterrupted draw.

The pub was reasonably lighted, but not overly bright. It was neither too close nor too open. Of this, at least, Bolan could approve; the contact had chosen well. He scanned the place as he and Rieck entered, assessing exits and examining, as casually as he could, the patrons within the bar. One man, sitting at a table in the corner with his back to the wall, was eyeing them intently. Bolan caught an almost imperceptible nod as Rieck and the seated man made eye contact. The two arrivals made their way to the man's table and sat down without introduction.

"Ziegler," the agent said by way of introduction.

"Rieck," he answered.

"I know." Ziegler nodded. "You had no trouble getting here?"

"None," Rieck said.

"You have not been told of my information?"

"No." Rieck stared at him. "Perhaps you should tell us what it is you want to tell us."

Ziegler nodded again. He was a gaunt man with a prominent Adam's apple and thinning black hair. He had pinched, almost pained features and small, close-set eyes. He wore a windbreaker over rumpled street clothes. If he carried a weapon, it wasn't apparent. There was a small wireless phone on the table in front of him, an advanced-looking model the soldier had never seen before. Ziegler nervously poked at it as he sat, sliding it around the surface of the table and moving it in circles.

Almost immediately Bolan didn't like the vibe he got from the Interpol contact. He'd been in the game long enough to know, however, that intelligence operatives quite often gave those around them the creeps. Staying in role camouflage for so long was bound to warp anyone's head and alter their mannerisms. There was no telling how long Ziegler had been in deep with Iron Thunder; no doubt he had to be half-mad to play along with Dumar Eon's vicious death cultists and not get caught.

"You need to understand," Ziegler said in low tones, "that Iron Thunder has been working toward a crescendo, of sorts." He looked left, then right, as if afraid someone might overhear. He lowered his voice even further. "This peak in their activities is coming very soon, Dumar Eon, their leader, is holding a rally today."

"In public?" Rieck asked.

"No," Ziegler shook his head furiously. "No, never. It is a secret location. A warehouse. I have the address here." He produced a folded slip of paper and passed it under the table. Bolan took it, glanced at it below the edge of the tabletop, and passed it over to Rieck. The Interpol operative read the address and then put the paper in his pocket.

"When?" Bolan asked.

"This afternoon, early this afternoon," Ziegler said. "If you hurry you can get there before it starts."

Bolan looked at his watch. They had burned through the morning with the shootout at the storage locker, not to mention its bureaucratic aftermath.

"No real time to set up a raid," Rieck said. "Not a properly organized one, anyway."

"No, no," Ziegler whispered. "You must not do that. If you raid them they will scatter, go underground. There will be no telling what they may do. But the rally… Iron Thunder's members must be led, must be directed. Dumar Eon will do this. I have been unable to learn their plans. These may be revealed at today's gathering."

"I wouldn't want to tell you how to do your job," Rieck said quietly, "but why would you not simply attend the rally in order to learn this, if it is revealed?"

"I cannot," Ziegler said. "I have other orders, standing orders. If I disobey, I risk exposure. But you, you could infiltrate. The rally will be very large. Iron Thunder chapters from all over the world will be represented. Such a large crowd, it will be easy to sneak in unnoticed. You could go and learn what they plan."

"It can't be that easy," Rieck said. "Just knowing the address won't get us in."

"No," Ziegler said. "It will not. You will need these. The black spot." He reached inside his windbreaker and removed two small index cards, each with a black circle inscribed on it. He passed these to Bolan and Rieck, again under the table, and the two men examined them. What at first looked like a solid black circle was in fact an elaborately and painstakingly drawn gothic design. The lines and whorls chased one after another in a seemingly endless series.

"This is a pass?" Bolan asked.

"Yes," Ziegler said. "Very difficult to forge. All of Iron Thunder's members have them. These were sent out through commercial courier to each chapter two weeks previously, with instructions on how to reach the rally. I have only just learned about it myself. Secrecy was very great. I was given one, which of course I cannot use. The other I stole from the jacket of another member, after one of the usual drinking bouts late last night." He waved his hand. "It is unimportant. But knowing you were assigned, and knowing he was here—" Ziegler indicated Bolan with a nod "—I took steps."

Bolan looked at Rieck.

"It would seem my activities within Interpol are public knowledge," the agent said grimly.

"The assassination attempt." Ziegler nodded. "I learned of this too late or I would have sent a warning. It is not known who might have betrayed you. I am pleased they did not get to you. I heard of the destruction at the coffee shop."

"To put it mildly," Rieck said.

"What do you know of the professional fighters in the Consortium's employ?" Bolan interjected. "We've faced Iron Thunder's members more than once, but also well-equipped, well-trained shooters, obviously professionals. These aren't Iron Thunder's rank and file, and they're not on the same page as the cultists. What's going on? What can you tell us?"

"I know no details," Ziegler said. "But there are rumors. The Consortium maintains a standing army, of sorts. Mercenaries, men who are paid to fight and to kill. They are not members of Iron Thunder. They are not under Dumar Eon's control, or so it is said, though they work for the company he has built. There is little interaction between the two. I do not think Iron Thunder's members trust them. They believe such men must be part of the Establishment, part of the old order of things. It is this order they believe they fight."

"So the right hand doesn't know what the left hand is doing," Bolan said.

Ziegler blinked at him.

"You're certain these passes are all we'll need to infiltrate the rally?" Rieck asked.

"Yes," he replied. "There will be so many members there, so many visitors from abroad. You will go unnoticed. Just two more invited representatives of Iron Thunder among the maddening crowd."

Bolan and Rieck exchanged glances.

"Well, I guess we're done here, then," Rieck said. He looked at Bolan again and the two men rose. Ziegler made no move to join them. Rieck nodded once, and they made their way from the pub. When the outside air hit them, Rieck breathed a sigh of relief.

"Don't get ahead of yourself," Bolan said.

"True." Rieck laughed. "I guess the real work is just starting."

Bolan drove the BMW as Rieck gave directions. "How much time have you spent undercover?" he asked the Interpol agent.

"Not much," Rieck admitted. "A few stings. Drug and weapons interdiction, that sort of thing. Nothing long-term."

"Move like you belong there. Fix your eyes on a point in front of you, beyond those nearest to you, and walk purposefully toward it as you move. Show no fear and no hesitation."

Rieck nodded.

They stopped at a shopping center and found an appropriate clothing store. When they had stowed their coats and Rieck's shoes in the trunk, they donned the items they'd purchased. Bolan's combat boots fit the role, and the large hooded sweatshirt he had found would cover his weapons adequately. Rieck had bought a pair of sneakers to replace his loafers, and had covered his button-down shirt with a gray sweatshirt. The sweatshirt bore a silk-screened quote that Bolan assumed was either funny or ironic. Rieck hadn't offered to translate it. Both men also bought hats and sunglasses. Rieck had a baseball cap and a pair of cheap shades, while Bolan's mirrored aviator lenses helped obscure his face. He wore a dark blue woolen watch cap.

It took some time to reach their destination, but the trip passed without incident. Bolan surveyed the area as he drove. He took a few passes around the block surrounding the address Ziegler had given them, satisfying himself as to the layout.

"There's one way in," he said, careful not to point in case someone was watching them. "That access road leads to the gate. No other exits, nothing on the opposite side. Once we're in, we're in until we leave their way. Keep that in mind."

"Understood," Rieck said.

The warehouse was deep in one of the city's industrial areas. There was a perimeter fence topped with straight rows of barbed wire strung between angled posts. The gate was open, but a pair of shaved-headed men in black flight jackets and combat boots loitered there, checking each car as it passed through. Bolan guided the BMW into the short queue of vehicles and waited patiently, all the while placing himself in the right frame of mind for the role he was about to play. Bolan was a master at role camouflage.

When it was their turn, he and Rieck both leaned toward the open driver's window. The larger of the two skinheads bent over, looking the BMW up and down before favoring Bolan with a gap-toothed smile. He said something in German.

Rieck replied for Bolan, saying something quickly and then following it with a lengthy monologue. The skinhead listened intently. Finally, his brow furrowed, and then he laughed. His friend joined in. Rieck reached into his coat and produced the paper pass Ziegler had provided. Bolan took the cue and did the same. The skinhead glanced at their cards, then waved them on.

"Drive in," Rieck whispered.

Bolan put his foot on the gas and let the BMW glide through the gate. "What was that all about?" he asked when they were clear.

"They wanted to know where we stole the car," the agent said. "I told them that it was, in fact, stolen, and told them an elaborate story about the lovely young lady we took it from.

"Are these…costumes going to be enough?" Rieck asked.

"If the crowd is big enough, they should be," Bolan said. "There may be some Iron Thunder members who know to look for you, or for both of us, but the ones who've seen us up close never came back. Those runners at the storage complex couldn't have studied us in too much detail. More importantly, they'll be focused on the rally."

The warehouse was surrounded by cars, parked two and three deep in concentric rings. Bolan picked a spot as close to the gate as possible and took the time to back in the BMW. This drew some honking horns from other drivers lining up around the building, but Bolan ignored them. His and Rieck's survival might well depend on being able to bull their way out of this mess of an impromptu parking lot.

"Not exactly low-key, is it?" The German watched through the windshield as Bolan eased the car into its spot.

"You can bet Iron Thunder, either on its own or through the Consortium's resources, has the local police locked in," Bolan speculated. "Bribes, intimidation… When you have their finances you can move the world."

"So what does that make you, Cooper?" Rieck managed a nervous grin. "The irresistible force or the immovable object?"

Bolan said nothing.

The Iron Thunder cultists milling about the parking lot and drifting in knots of two or more to the double doors of the warehouse entrance ranged widely in age and appearance. Most were in their twenties, but there were a few teenagers, quite a few middle-aged men and women, and a surprising number of senior citizens. They wore all manner of dress, from street tough getups to business suits, and everything in between. Bolan saw no firearms, but that meant nothing. Here and there were telltale bulges beneath clothing. A few of the rougher-looking cultists carried chains or clubs, and he saw one leather-clad woman carrying a bullwhip. On the whole, though, the people before him seemed far more interested in getting inside the warehouse for the rally than in any immediate aggression.

As he and Rieck fell in with the crowd and walked casually toward the double doors, Bolan pondered the throngs about him. What sort of message appealed to such a wide range of people? He had seen his share of cult leaders and charismatic figureheads, certainly. Most of them appealed only to certain stripes, people with a shared need. What shared need did all of these people have? What was the attraction in the death cult's nihilistic message? Perhaps the rally itself would answer some of those questions.

If not, it wouldn't matter. Bolan's mission was to get to the roots of Iron Thunder and the Consortium, and, ultimately, to burn them to the ground. Brognola had made the pro forma request for information, for damning or incriminating evidence, but Bolan was no police officer. He was a soldier, and he did a soldier's job. The big Fed knew that, too. Bolan would learn what he needed to learn about Iron Thunder and the Consortium, yes, and he would follow the trail of slime back to the source. Then it would be time to plug the security holes the two groups represented.

Permanently.

The crowd grew as they filed through the doors. Inside, the warehouse was a simple and typical concrete-and-metal enclosure. High ceilings were held in place by metal beams, among which small, agitated birds flitted. While it was brisk outside, the heat within the warehouse was palpable, generated by the hundreds of rally attendees.

The light was dim, and the high-set windows of the warehouse had been spray-painted black to keep out the gray daylight. What illumination there was came from flickering torches set at intervals along the walls. At the far end of the warehouse was a large, rough-hewn stage that looked cobbled together from scrap wood. This was dominated by a podium and, behind it, a giant screen. The projector was switched on and the screen was filled by a projected silhouette: a sledgehammer and a chainsaw, bright white light in a circle of black.

From somewhere, probably hidden beneath the podium, speakers blared the first few notes of a popular heavy metal song. This was signal enough to the crowds, who ceased their chatter and looked up at the stage. Bolan glanced left and right, at the people standing shoulder to shoulder around him and Rieck. They were absolutely rapt in their focus, one or two almost catatonic with joy as they waited. Bolan examined them for as long as he dared, careful to keep his head and his mirrored sunglasses pointed toward the podium. When he sensed movement on the stage, he, too, focused on the platform.

The recorded heavy metal music reached a crescendo and increased in volume as a figure appeared. The long-haired man, dressed in a tailored suit and wearing black leather gloves on his hands, had the physique of a bodybuilder beneath the almost straining fabric. He wore expensive sunglasses over his eyes, and he walked with the grace of a panther. The man strode to the podium, allowing the projected logo behind him to backlight him. The effect created a halo about him, intensified by small LED lights in the podium that cast shadows from beneath his jaw.

The music cut out completely. The sudden silence within the warehouse was ominous. The crowd, as one, held its collective breath.

Dumar Eon was about to speak.

9

Dumar Eon stood before the podium, looking out over the assembled followers. It was hard to tell behind the sunglasses, but Bolan thought Dumar's gaze passed directly over him and Rieck. The man worked the crowd without saying a word, the touch of his eyes a kind of blessing of which the Iron Thunder cultists seemed only too aware. One young woman fainted, and the crowd closed in around her; Eon smiled at that.

At his hand signal, Eon's image was projected simultaneously on the screen behind him. It moved with a minute but perceptible delay. The effect was mesmerizing, as the trailing image loomed larger than life behind the man it mimicked.

"Welcome," Eon said finally. He spoke in English, and German subtitles appeared on the screen behind him. Bolan wondered about that for a moment, but then realized it was probably the closest thing to a common language the international membership of the cult was likely to have.

Microphones, possibly in the podium, picked up Eon's voice, amplifying it, distorting it electronically and creating a deliberate echo effect. This was similar to the voice changer Eon used in many of his propaganda videos. The faithful went insane, stomping their feet and clapping their hands. Bolan and Rieck imitated those around them.

"What is there to love about this world?"

The crowd screamed in response. "Nothing!"

"What is there to leave in this world?"

"Nothing!" they shouted in unison.

"What can you expect anyone to do for you?"

"Nothing!"

"That is right!" Eon shouted back. "Nothing! The world is an empty, miserable place. It is pain. It is boredom. It is endless, crushing, mindless work. Nations rise and nations fall, and still the crushing misery goes on! The world economy? A shambles! Wars among nations? Never ending! Pestilence, famine, apathy…everywhere! What can be done to solve these problems?"

"Nothing!" the crowd bellowed.

"Nothing," Eon repeated. "Nothing at all. The beauty of this nothing is that nothing is also the solution to your pain. It is the wonderful, beautiful nothing of beyond, toward which we reach, toward which we strive. Will you join me in nothing?"

"Yes!" the crowd roared.

"We stand at a precipice," Eon said. He paused and looked down, allowing the pause to grow, to dominate. His audience grew silent, and the cult leader finally continued. He spread his arms wide. "A vast and mighty chasm that leaves us with no alternatives. We cannot back up, for the bridges have been fired as we crossed them. We cannot turn away, for this brings us no farther forward. No, to progress, to do more, to be more, to continue, we must move onward! Into the chasm! Unto the breach! And you, the few who have the eyes to see, the wisdom to know, the courage to *be,* you, Iron Thunder, will take that step into the abyss! We will carry the torches that show the way! We will be the genesis of a bold new age, in which the gift we bring, the joy we share, the end we love is fully acknowledged by all."

Eon paused. He began to pace the stage, his voice no less augmented as he went on. Bolan could hear the rustle of the man's suit as he walked; he was wearing a wireless microphone.

"You all know the gift I bring, the gift I preach and the gift we will encourage others to accept. That is the gift of sweet, blissful release from terrestrial pain. It is the gift of oblivion. It is, in its most vulgar expression, the gift of *death*. But we cannot call it that, not commonly. It is so much more, and the word itself carries such negative associations. We must make the masses embrace the gift of oblivion as we have. We must make them *understand*." Dumar Eon walked back and forth like a caged animal, like a man possessed. He radiated energy. Bolan raised his estimation of Eon's abilities. This was an incredibly dangerous man who could hold the attention—and the devotion—of hundreds of followers, and those followers were willing to kill and to die for their leader.

Eon returned to the podium. He put his hands on either side of it as if it were the only thing in the world, as if this simple piece of furniture held him up. He sank in place, almost imperceptibly. Bolan had to hand it to him—he knew how to play an audience, right down to the body language that reinforced his words so subtly and effectively. With a flourish, he removed his sunglasses.

Behind Eon, the image being projected zoomed closer and closer, until only his eyes were visible. "My friends," he said, "my dear, dear friends, my closest family, my blood brothers and sisters… For so very long we have lived in the shadows, worked in the shadows, brought our joy to others in the shadows. I have called you all here today, called you here on this momentous, glorious day, to tell you that the shadows are growing shorter. Night is yielding to the sun. It is time that we bring the greatest pleasure to the greatest number in a way that tells the world, the entire world, the mainstream world, that we exist. No longer will they ignore us. No longer will we be dismissed. No longer will the gift be spurned."

"I don't like where this is going," Rieck whispered, just loudly enough for Bolan to hear.

"I know," Eon said, "I know that you have all been waiting impatiently! Since the presents I sent you circled the globe, arriving at your doorsteps or in the secret places only you trust, I know you have been waiting. You need wait no longer! For if Iron Thunder has meant anything, if it has been anything, it has done so while marching hand in hand with technology. It is technology that will link us as we march forward into this bold new world, allowing us to synchronize our most critical movements, our most profound operations. Through technology we will set ourselves apart and bring ourselves together. Through technology we will rule the world. But first I have a call to make."

Eon removed a small object from inside his suit jacket. He flipped it open. It was a very small, very modern-looking wireless phone. Bolan realized instantly where he had seen such a phone. It had been sitting on the table in front of Ziegler.

"No longer must you be content to receive messages from me, and from each other, through the Internet. No longer must you wonder which unworthy souls could be reading what you share. No longer must you fear that your connection with your fellow members of Iron Thunder is vulnerable. No longer will it be indirect. The very special phones you all have will keep you connected at all times, and each phone incorporates special scrambling technology that will keep it secure."

Rieck looked at Bolan worriedly. Bolan shook his head minutely.

"Now," Eon said from the stage, "you will receive the first of what will be many communiqués from me. You will see

how well our network operates. You will raise your phones
to the skies with me, and you will voice your triumph, for we
are Iron Thunder! We will burn the world!"

"We will burn the world!" the cultists began to chant in
unison. "We will burn the world! We will burn the world!"

Eon pressed a button on his phone. Around Rieck and
Bolan, cultists began reacting as their own phones reacted.
As each man and woman opened his or her phone, the stylized logo of Iron Thunder appeared on the small color screen.
Each cultist raised that phone high overhead. The chanting,
the foot-stomping, the wave and wall of hyperactive crowd
energy washed over the multitudes assembled to pay obeisance
to Dumar Eon.

One of the cultists turned to Bolan and then looked at
Rieck. *"Wo sind ihre telefone?"* he asked.

"Uh-oh," Rieck said.

Bolan braced himself.

"Stop!" Eon said from the stage. The crowd, so deafening a
moment before, went silent in a heartbeat. Mack Bolan stood
his ground, flexing his hands subtly and dropping very slightly
into a crouch. His muscles were coiled and ready for action.
He was very aware of the hundreds of cultists now turning to
face him and the Interpol agent, as Eon pointed an imperious
finger at the pair.

"Those two!" Eon said from the stage, his distorted voice
echoing over the sound system. "Clear a path!" He reached
for his lapel and switched off his wireless microphone.

The cultists parted like an enchanted sea. Eon jumped
from the stage, landing among them with easy grace. He
pointed again at the two intruders and walked slowly along
the cleared path. The cultists who were not fixed on Bolan and
Rieck followed Eon's movements with silent and wide-eyed
absorption.

Eon stopped scant paces in front of Bolan. He glanced at Rieck, but then looked back to Bolan again. He gestured at his face.

Bolan slowly removed his sunglasses.

"You," Eon said. "The American. And that one—" he indicated Rieck with a jerk of his chin "—Adam Rieck, Interpol."

"Word gets around," Bolan said.

"It does," Eon agreed. "We've known of your existence since the first night."

"I left you a pile of bodies." Bolan shrugged. "Are you saying your vast intelligence network ferreted that out?"

"Please, please," Eon said, frowning. "There is no need to be vulgar. We are all civilized men, Mr.…." He paused for Bolan to give his name.

"That will do." Bolan smiled faintly.

"No matter," Eon said. He sounded mildly irritated. "We could learn your name if we wished."

"Now who's being vulgar?" Bolan asked.

Eon sighed. "True," he said. "We could learn your cover identity, I suppose. Are you CIA? Your kind so often is CIA."

"Had a lot of experience in that department, have you?" Bolan asked.

"Please," Eon said again. "I've asked you to be civilized. I'm quite certain, based on what little I know of you, that were you not surrounded by hundreds of enemies you'd be fighting your way out right now."

Bolan said nothing.

"Yes, well," Eon continued, "let us not dwell on that. Let us simply take it as given that there are dozens of guns trained on you right now, and those guns are quite unnecessary. At a single word from me, the men and women surrounding you at this moment would gladly rend you limb from limb. You understand this, yes?"

"Yes," Bolan said.

"Good. You will come quietly, then. You will make no attempt to reach for your weapons. Your friend will likewise accept his fate passively. Both of you will be conducted from this place and taken to a more secure location. Should you refuse, you will be horribly, brutally killed on this very spot and, while I know you will take a few of my people with you, I assure you that they would go to their deaths with gratitude on their lips—and your flesh in their teeth. Do you wish to resist?"

"Let's say I choose my battles," Bolan said.

"Oh, yes, let us say that," Eon laughed. His expression hardened instantly and he snapped his fingers. Several hulking male cultists, more skinheads, appeared from the throng as if by magic.

"Ja," one of them said.

"These men," Eon said, "are not true believers." The skinheads nodded and circled the soldier and the agent. Three produced handguns, while a fourth snapped open a switchblade.

"We're also not very smart," Rieck said abruptly. "You were expecting us, weren't you?"

It was Eon's turn to smile and say nothing. Finally, he glanced at Bolan, and again frowned. "You have nothing you wish to say to me?"

"Like what?" Bolan asked.

"I don't know. A confession of your crimes? Pleas for mercy? Threats that you represent a powerful government agency within a powerful nation? Vows that I will never get away with this? Dire promises of vengeance? Anything?"

"You've been watching too much television," Bolan said calmly.

Eon blinked. "Indeed. Perhaps I have." He moved in close, speaking in low tones at the side of Bolan's head, as if whispering into his ear. "You do realize, American, that I will torture both of you until you scream to tell me what you know."

"Your kind usually does," Bolan said, without turning to look at the cult leader directly. "What is it you think we know?"

"You have a point," Eon admitted. "In truth, I know as much about you as I need to know. I know you are interfering in Iron Thunder, most likely because Interpol thinks it has uncovered some of my less noble actions with regard to our host country. Is that general enough? Yes, I think it is."

"So why torture us?"

"Why not?" Eon said earnestly. "The gift will be that much sweeter when it finally comes to you. I dare say even one such as you would welcome it, by then."

"I've seen it before," Bolan said.

"Have you? Have you, now?" Eon looked Bolan in the eyes, locking his gaze with the soldier's. Something he saw in Bolan's expression, perhaps, caused him to break the stare.

"Seen it. It was no 'gift.' It was just the brutal end to a brutal act. Everybody paid."

"Such tragically outdated sensibilities." Eon sniffed. "But yes. I can see it in your eyes. You have seen death. You have taken life. Many times, I suspect."

Bolan again said nothing.

"I wish I could be there to witness it personally," Eon said finally. "But I have too much to do. I have certain business matters to which I must attend, certain weeds in the garden of Eden that must be pulled."

"I don't mind waiting while you get caught up," Bolan offered.

Eon stopped, blinked and laughed again. It wasn't a pleasant sound. "A good try!" He rattled off a series of instructions in German, pointing to the skinheads and gesticulating wildly. The cultists nodded repeatedly and seized Rieck and Bolan by the arms.

"Do you really want to make yourself known to Interpol like this?" Rieck asked. "Think it over, Eon. You kill me and the international law-enforcement community will never stop coming."

"You poor, naive fool," Eon said. "Nobody will ever find you. And nobody will ever be able to prove that I have brought you oblivion."

He turned to Bolan again. "As for you, I will have your torture videotaped. It will be a special pleasure for me. Please do your best. I want to enjoy it for as long as possible. Perhaps I will edit the best parts together and share it with my people. Take heart, American. You are about to become famous. You will live forever, and beyond death."

"You first," Bolan said. It wasn't a threat. It wasn't a promise. Bolan could have been speaking of the weather. His words were simple, final and factual. He believed it. Eon, too, could see this.

"Goodbye, American," he said.

"Yeah," Bolan answered. He and Rieck were led away by the skinheads, as the anxious and horribly silent crowd watched every inch of their walk out of the warehouse.

Bolan wasn't surprised. These things happened; these risks were very real.

It was going to be a long afternoon.

10

Bolan opened his eyes.

The ache in his skull, a familiar one, told him all he needed to know. One of the skinheads had blackjacked him, probably the moment they got out of reach of the hundreds of cultists they were leaving behind at the warehouse. Eon was smart, and he knew danger when he saw it. He was obviously taking no chances.

As he had done many times before, Bolan assessed himself without moving. He flexed his fingers, his toes; he stretched in place, gently at first, then with more tension. He didn't believe he was injured, except for the ache in his skull. That would fade quickly enough.

Bolan was on his side, with his hands restrained behind his back. He tested the bonds on his wrists again; they gave slightly and felt slick. Duct tape. His ankles were similarly taped. Without a sound, he pushed himself to a sitting position.

His weapons were gone, as was the hooded sweatshirt he had worn over them. His captors hadn't taken his boots, but they had made a thorough search of the pockets of his combat blacksuit. The garment resembled black battle dress utilities, but was a bit less baggy. With effort, he checked the secret pockets sewn into the lining of his clothes, but the small escape knife and the wire garrote had been found and removed.

The wall behind his back was cold and rough, a simple cinder block construction. Peeling green paint coated the room. There was no furniture, and no windows. A single door, of metal with a heavy steel latch handle, faced him. Across the room, lying prone against the wall, was Rieck. He wasn't moving. His sweatshirt was gone, but he still had his sneakers and looked otherwise unharmed. Bolan imagined they'd knocked him cold, too. It was a messy business, really, striking a man in the head to knock him out. There was a good chance he'd wake up with a concussion, if he woke up at all. Bolan had met several sap-happy criminals during his endless war, and blackjacking prisoners was especially popular among the Mafia types. He couldn't say he'd missed it.

The soldier crabbed his way across the floor until he was next to Rieck. He reached from behind his back, awkwardly, to get two fingers against the man's neck. The pulse was steady and strong. Bolan rolled so he could face the agent, and kicked the man's feet with his own boots. Rieck stirred.

"Hey," Bolan said. "Hey, Rieck. Wake up."

The agent opened his eyes and immediately squeezed them shut, groaning loudly. "God! What happened?"

"Ever held a lead-lined leather sap?" Bolan said.

"No."

"Well, you've felt the business end of one," he commented. "How do you feel?"

"My head hurts like mad."

"Beyond the obvious," Bolan said.

Rieck took a moment to consider. "Nothing major, I suppose."

"No nausea? Blurry vision? Anything like that?"

Get FREE BOOKS and a FREE GIFT when you play the...

LAS VEGAS

GAME

Just scratch off the gold box with a coin. Then check below to see the gifts you get!

YES! I have scratched off the gold box. Please send me my **2 FREE BOOKS** and **gift for which I qualify**. I understand that I am under no obligation to purchase any books as explained on the back of this card.

◄ **DETACH AND MAIL CARD TODAY!** ▼

366 ADL E373   166 ADL E373

FIRST NAME   LAST NAME

ADDRESS

APT.#   CITY

STATE / PROV.   ZIP/POSTAL CODE

| 7 | 7 | 7 | Worth TWO FREE BOOKS plus a BONUS Mystery Gift! |

Worth TWO FREE BOOKS!

TRY AGAIN!

Offer limited to one per household and not valid to current subscribers of Gold Eagle® books. All orders subject to approval. Please allow 4 to 6 weeks for delivery.

The Reader Service — Here's how it works:

Accepting your 2 free books and free gift (gift valued at approximately $5.00) places you under no obligation to buy anything. You may keep the books and gift and return the shipping statement marked "cancel." If you do not cancel, about a month later we'll send you 6 additional books and bill you just $31.94* — that's a savings of 24% off the cover price of all 6 books! And there's no extra charge for shipping! You may cancel at any time, but if you choose to continue, every other month we'll send you 6 more books, which you may either purchase at the discount price or return to us and cancel your subscription.

*Terms and prices subject to change without notice. Price does not include applicable taxes. Sales tax applicable in N.Y. Canadian residents will be charged applicable provincial taxes and GST. Offer not vaid in Quebec. Credit or debit balances in a customer's account(s) may be offset by any other outstanding balance owed by or to the customer. Offer available while quantities last.

BUSINESS REPLY MAIL
FIRST-CLASS MAIL   PERMIT NO. 717   BUFFALO, NY

POSTAGE WILL BE PAID BY ADDRESSEE

THE READER SERVICE
PO BOX 1867
BUFFALO NY 14240-9952

NO POSTAGE
NECESSARY
IF MAILED
IN THE
UNITED STATES

"No, nothing like that," Rieck said. He looked around. His ankles and wrists were taped, too, though his arms were bound in front of his body rather than behind his back. "Cooper, where are we?"

Bolan considered that. The room was far too large to be a storage closet, but the simple box construction and lack of windows meant it had to be some sort of industrial space.

"Not far, I think," Bolan said. "Probably someplace convenient to the warehouse." Twisting his neck, he caught a glimpse of his wrist, to find his watch was gone.

"Mine, too," Rieck said, making a face. "And my wallet. They took everything."

"Not everything," Bolan said. "Be glad they left you your sneakers. I've seen amateurs who were smart enough to take them."

"I'd hate to meet anyone you considered professional," Rieck muttered, holding his head.

Bolan ignored that and pushed himself to his feet. He hopped around the cell, using the wall to steady himself, feeling for any break in the cinder blocks. He also examined the ceiling, looking for microphone pickups and cameras. There didn't appear to be anything, though that was no guarantee.

"What now?" Rieck asked.

"Nothing, for the moment," Bolan said. "Sooner or later that door opens." He nodded at the metal door and then tapped on it. It was speckled with rust and felt very solid.

"And then?"

"Then the rough stuff starts," he said. "You heard the man."

"I was hoping he was just trying to scare us."

Bolan said nothing. He was eyeing one of the hinges on the door.

"What do you see?" Rieck asked.

"Rust," Bolan said. "A lot of rust. Enough to make that hinge abrasive." He backed up against the door and started to saw away with his wrists, rubbing the duct tape back and forth across the hinge as quickly as he could.

"This will take a while," Bolan said. "But I might be able to get it started. When they come, it's very important that you keep them occupied."

"That's touching of you, Cooper." Rieck laughed bitterly.

"It's a rough deal." Bolan nodded. "But I can get us out of here, if you give me enough time."

"I'll do my best."

There was no way to know if they were being monitored or if the cultists had been checking them periodically, but they did come. The group who entered the makeshift prison was the same bunch of skinheads. They were joined by a man in a tailored gray business suit. His head was bald, and he wore small, round, wire-rimmed glasses. His beard was neatly trimmed.

"Ah, good," he said in English. His accent was thick, but he was understandable. He was looking at Bolan as he spoke. "Are you ready, American?"

Bolan had planted himself against the wall when he heard the keys hit the door lock outside. He looked up, giving no indication that he was testing the strength of the mangled duct tape still covering his wrists.

"For?" he asked, sounding bored.

"Why, to watch your friend scream," the man said cheerfully. He snapped his fingers, and two of the skinheads took Rieck by the arms. A third disappeared through the open doorway, only to return with a wooden chair. He put the chair in the center of the room and spit a command in German. The skinheads planted Rieck on the seat, holding him upright and immobile.

Bolan ticked off the numbers. There was the man in the suit, and a total of five shaved-headed street toughs. Not bad odds at all, considering, but he would need some sort of equalizer to take them all quickly enough. The skinheads displayed no weapons and didn't appear to be carrying any, though it was hard to say who might have a pair of brass knuckles, a .25-caliber pistol, or a flick-knife tucked away in a pocket.

"My name is Finn," the suited man said. "I am, how would you call it, a group leader within Iron Thunder. I am very pleased to have been given this assignment." He spoke another command, and the skinhead who had been hanging back in the doorway removed a small digital Flip camera from his jacket. He pointed it at Rieck and pressed a button.

"You're not going to put naked pictures of me on the Internet, I hope," Rieck said.

Finn looked annoyed. "Do not waste my time, *policeman,*" he said, his voice thick with contempt. "I have none to spare for your false courage. I have questions. You have answers. We will proceed swiftly and efficiently. Your friend there will watch, to see what awaits him, and when you die horribly, screaming for us to kill you to end the pain, he will know that there is no release but our sweet gift of oblivion, and he will tell us what we want to know."

"Your boss thinks there isn't anything we can tell you," Rieck said. He was pale, but his voice held. Bolan watched with respect, straining silently against the duct tape. The man had guts.

"Tell us everything that Interpol knows about Iron Thunder," Finn said. "Tell us now. And tell us why this American is involved, and what he is likely to know."

"It's a big file," Rieck said. "I forget."

"Tell us now!" Finn shouted. He pointed, and one of the skinheads holding Rieck cuffed him hard in the side of the head, bloodying the Interpol agent's ear.

"Ow," Rieck said.

"Again! Again!" Finn demanded.

The skinheads needed no further urging. They began taking turns punching and battering Rieck, using their elbows, their knuckles and their open palms. Rieck grunted with each blow but otherwise took it silently.

Bolan felt the duct tape on his wrists begin to give way.

"Enough," Finn said. He looked at Bolan, then back to Rieck. "I can see this impresses neither of you. Nor did I expect it to make much difference. But we had to see just how soft he might be, *nein?*"

"Fuck you," Rieck said, spitting blood. His lip was split in several places and was starting to swell.

"Ah, good, still some spirit." Finn reached into the pocket of his slacks. His hand came back out with an expensive, lever-actuated automatic knife. The stainless-steel blade snapped open at a press of the lever.

Bolan had his equalizer.

"Now," Finn said, "I am done playing with you. American." He didn't take his eyes from Rieck as he spoke to Bolan. "I am going to carve out each of your friend's eyes. I am, as you say, cutting to the chase." He laughed. "You see? I make a joke in your language. But if you want to stop me from blinding him, you must tell me everything you know. Only that will save you."

"You don't want that," Bolan said. He had his plan now. A lot hinged on his timing and on the brutality with which he could execute that plan.

"What?" Finn looked puzzled.

"We both know you don't want any information," Bolan said. "You want us to refuse to talk. You want a copy of the video your friend there is taking. You want to sit alone late at night and watch it over and over again."

"Brave words." Finn forced a laugh. "Now I cut your friend until he screams to die."

"Sure, sure," Bolan taunted. "Posture and wave your knife around. We both know what you're after. Admit it. You get kinky sexual thrills from all this. I know why you've saved me for last, too. You're going to send the cue balls there out of the room—" Bolan nodded to the skinheads "—so you can get me alone. Then you're going to tell me how nice you can be to me, if only I do a few obscene favors for you."

One of the skinheads took the bait. He elbowed his buddy and the two started talking and laughing in German. Finn turned on them, shouting something that was probably a demand that they shut up.

Keep the pressure on, Bolan thought to himself. Get him mad enough to shut you up himself. He'll want to take a stab at you to show he's not weak.

"You," Finn said, "will be quiet before I cut your tongue out."

"We both know you won't do that," Bolan said. He favored one of the skinheads with an exaggerated wink, which brought more harsh laughter from the man and his friends.

"Enough!" Finn shouted. He whirled on Bolan, bringing the knife in low. His intent was clear. He was going to put that blade in the big American.

Bolan waited until the last possible second, feigning a look of shock and fear that was all the impetus Finn needed to keep coming. When the blade was inches from his face, it was time.

The Executioner struck.

He moved like a rattler, the knife edges of his freed hands shooting out to chop Finn in either side of his neck. The brutal, scissoring blows brought the man up short. Bolan rolled his left arm and elbow, moving Finn down and sideways, scooping the open switchblade out of his hand. In the same movement he slashed the tape holding his ankles together, feeling the blade take a chunk out of the skin of his ankle, but ignoring the minor wound. The shocked skinheads were only starting to move, only beginning to react, when Bolan surged to his feet and kicked the closest one in the knee.

The man screamed and folded on the shattered kneecap. Bolan vaulted him and slashed the knife across the throat of the second man. The skinhead with the camera was beginning to drop his digital recorder and reach for something in his waistband. Bolan snapped a palm heel into his face and followed with a brutal knee blow to the groin.

The men who had been holding Rieck moved from the agent and rushed at Bolan. The first executed a clumsy tackle, taking the big American to the ground and landing on top of him. Bolan, prepared for the impact, made sure to keep his arms free of the skinhead's bear hug. He simply drove the bloody knife into his adversary's neck, then rolled out from under the dying man.

The last skinhead had drawn a pistol.

The Walther P-99 was an expensive piece of hardware for a street thug, but Bolan wasn't interested in the weapon's provenance. The thug, perhaps never having fired it before, hesitated just a second before his finger closed on the trigger. It was all the time Bolan needed to slap the gun sideways and yank at his arm, driving the web of his free hand into the gunman's throat. The pistol went off and the skinhead collapsed to the floor, choking while Bolan pried the smoking Walther from his hand.

He whipped around again, facing the door, knowing the numbers were falling and his time was running out. Men had come running, yet more of the skinheads on whom Dumar Eon seemed to rely for security. Bolan shot the first one through the head and snapped a clean chest shot into the second. He watched as both men hit the floor outside the improvised cell. Then he checked the Walther to verify the remaining ammunition, stuck his head out the doorway quickly, then looked a second time to make sure no one was coming.

"Nothing," he said simply.

Rieck spit blood. "Cooper," he said, "could you untie me, please?" He sounded a bit awed. There was little to be particularly impressed with, to Bolan's thinking; amateurs like that were easily enough taken down. It took time to wade through them, but wasn't really difficult. The problem was that any idiot with a gun or a knife could get lucky. The Executioner's foes had to get lucky only once; he had burned through what he imagined were his nine lives long ago, on countless battlefields around the globe.

Bolan surveyed the fallen skinheads. They weren't all dead, but none of them would be getting up anytime soon. One of the men was groaning quietly. Bolan made sure he wasn't aware enough to draw a hidden weapon, then retrieved the switchblade he had tossed aside when the Walther presented itself. Tucking the pistol in his waistband, he wiped the knife's blade on Finn's suit jacket and then used it to cut the duct tape securing Rieck.

"Thanks," the Interpol agent said thickly.

"How are you holding up?" Bolan asked, searching Finn's pockets.

"I'll live," Rieck said.

"Then give me a hand searching these men," Bolan said. "And keep your ears out for anyone else approaching. I'm assuming that gunshot would have brought anyone with an interest in what's going on here. They shouldn't give much trouble now, but if anybody looks conscious, kick him in the head."

"It will be a pleasure," Rieck said.

Most of what the skinheads carried was junk or personal effects, not worth taking. Rieck pocketed a pair of brass knuckles one of them had toted; Bolan imagined the agent was looking forward to a little payback for his afternoon beating. Finn had been carrying one of the special phones. Bolan took it.

"It seems Ziegler failed to mention that," Rieck said bitterly.

Bolan nodded. "Looks that way."

"He's the leak," Rieck said. "The reason Iron Thunder's known what to expect all along. There's no telling how long he's been planted within Interpol. Probably awhile, if Dumar Eon is the kind of forward thinker he presents himself to be."

Bolan covered their withdrawal with the Walther. They found themselves in an outbuilding that, when they looked through one of the grimy windows, turned out to be adjacent to the warehouse. On a card table by the door, Bolan found his weapons and gear, as well as Rieck's personal effects and his MP-5 K. Bolan's canvas war bag was under the card table. He looked through it quickly, satisfied that nothing was missing, and pocked the BMW keys, which had been in the pile of goods.

"Looks like they searched the car," Bolan said. He looked out one filth-encrusted window, then another. Finally, he spotted the vehicle. The trunk was still open. "Got it."

"Not very good at this, were they?" Rieck grinned.

"No, not really," Bolan admitted. He tossed over the car keys. "You drive."

"No rest for the weary." Rieck sighed.

"None at all."

11

The parking garage was dark and close. David Schucker sat in the back of his Mercedes, watching the shadows cast by the inadequate light fixtures. He wasn't pleased by this meeting location, which afforded far too many hiding places. While he would never admit it, a recurring nightmare for him was to be surrounded, abruptly, by law-enforcement officials bent on seeing him behind bars. This was absurd, he knew, for the Consortium was well practiced at paying the right people to ensure that this did happen. But it bothered him nonetheless, the very idea of it. He wouldn't go to prison. Not at his age. And he couldn't live in a cage after sampling the good life. It simply wasn't in him.

He put the thoughts out of his mind as he looked at the face of the expensive gold watch on his wrist. It wouldn't do to psych himself out, he scolded mentally, just when a show of strength was necessary. Bashir was an animal who respected nothing *but* strength. If he thought for a moment he could take the chemicals without paying, he would do so. He would also have no compunctions about turning around and using the deadly nerve agents and other chemical weapons on the very country where he'd purchased them; it was the sort of thing that appealed to his barbarous streak, if Schucker was any judge.

This was of no concern to Schucker himself, however. He would empty the bank accounts of petty would-be dictators like Assan Bashir for as long as he could, and when he was sitting on a fortune that was as large as he could make it, he would retire. The key was in the balancing act: squeezing as much cash from the buyers as one could, while avoiding the legal repercussions for selling to them what the Consortium shouldn't have been manufacturing without license anyway. The vertical integration of the Consortium's various holdings made it all possible, and Schucker's security force helped keep a tight rein on potential leaks while violently removing any would-be interlopers. Some of the Consortium's lesser operations, for example, such as the manufacture of designer hallucinogens and synthetic "speed" for domestic and world markets, had been attacked by rival drug traffickers in the past. Schucker's trained and experienced mercenaries had made short work of them, and done so violently enough for the eliminations to serve as object lessons to other such competitors.

Some distance from Schucker's car were three cargo vehicles. Gunnar Heinriksen and a team of security operatives stood guard over the three panel trucks, which contained the contents of the secured storage area that had been emptied on his order. This overt act would surely draw Dumar Eon's attention, eventually, if the man ever bothered to check the stockpiles. If he was planning some cataclysmic event to spread his death cult's message, he would check sooner rather than later. Schucker had advanced the timetable because of that, and he had dealt with considerable complaining from Bashir as a result. The Syrian, who was some sort of heir to power in his native land, was a petulant and stubborn man. He liked things to occur on his terms, and disliked being told when and where to appear. Schucker has placated him by reducing the asking price, which was still very handsome. Some part of that galled Schucker, but he suppressed it as he did most such emotions. There was no room for regret or resentment; it was enough that the sale was made.

The handheld radio on the seat next to Schucker crackled as one of his men keyed his own unit. "The car is here," the voice said in German. "We are following."

Schucker nodded to himself. All was proceeding according to plan. His men would follow Bashir's car up from the entrance level, and they would stand off at a discreet distance with their weapons ready. There was little chance the Syrians would attempt a double cross, but when dealing with such individuals, Schucker believed in taking all possible precautions.

The limousine pulled slowly into position. Schucker stepped out of his car and moved forward into the small circle of light afforded by one of the fluorescent overheads. He waited for some time. He had expected this; Bashir would make him wait in payment for forcing the Syrian to change his schedule and arrive earlier than originally agreed, when the sale of the weapons had first been brokered. Schucker endured this childishness, knowing that provoking Bashir could only make matters worse and prolong the exchange further.

Finally, the doors of the limousine opened. Several large men in expensive suits climbed from the car. They brandished small submachine guns of a type Schucker didn't recognize. No doubt they were the latest thing, and very expensive. For Assan Bashir, only the best would do.

Schucker was dimly aware of Bashir's aspirations. There was some sort of power play among those in line for the throne, or the presidency, or whatever the Syrians had that constituted their government. It was all so incredibly *boring* that Schucker forced himself to be deliberately ignorant of it. It was his way of marginalizing beasts like Bashir in his mind. Regardless, possession of the proverbial "weapons of mass destruction" that the Consortium could offer him would give

Bashir the leverage he needed to accomplish his goals—or at least Bashir thought so. Schucker didn't care if the man attained his vision of power or not, as long as he paid.

Finally, Bashir deigned to make an appearance. He was dressed much like his men, though his fingers were dripping with gold and diamond-inset rings. He was shorter and squatter than his security people, with a wide face and broad cheeks. His eyes were a mystery, for Schucker had never seen them. Bashir affected a pair of sunglasses at all times. The lenses were so dark that no hint of the eyes behind them ever showed.

"Assan," Schucker said obsequiously. He spoke in English because it was a language they shared. "Thank you for gracing me with your presence."

Bashir waved one pudgy hand. "Spare me your false pleasantries, David," he said. "Let us not waste time with lies and shows of affection."

Schucker's face hardened. "Very well, Assan. You have the money?"

"I have the money." Bashir motioned to his guards. One of them went to the limousine's trunk and, very slowly, removed a briefcase from it. Bashir smiled, looking past the vehicle to the darkness of the parking garage.

"Something distracts you, Assan?" Schucker asked.

"Again, you waste my time with pretense," Bashir said. "Your men are not as invisible as they believe. I know they are there. I know you have instructed them to shoot me if you think we mean to betray you."

Schucker shrugged. "It is what you would do."

Bashir looked at him. His thick lips parted in a toothy smile. His teeth were capped and seemed too large for his mouth. "Yes," he said, chuckling. "Yes, it is what I would do." He spoke a word in his native tongue and the guard brought the briefcase forward. He presented it to Schucker, who took it, placed it on the hood of the Mercedes and opened it.

The bills inside were crisp and neatly stacked. Schucker suppressed a smile. He snapped the briefcase shut.

"I will take my merchandise now," Bashir commanded.

It was Schucker's turn to motion for an underling. At his gesture, Heinriksen approached and held out three sets of keys. Without prompting, Bashir's men took them. Heinriksen pointed each man to the correct vehicle. The Syrian drivers stepped forward, two to a truck. The engines started up almost before the doors were closed.

"We are done here," Bashir said. He climbed back into his limousine without another word. The limo slowly turned in the space available and then disappeared down the ramp, followed by the panel trucks. The smell of exhaust lingered in the air.

"All is in order, sir?" Heinriksen asked. He pointed to the briefcase.

"Yes, Gunnar, stop worrying," Schucker said dismissively. He handed him the case. "Let's get out of here."

One of the guards began shouting animatedly.

"What the hell is that?" Schucker said.

"I'll go see, sir," Heinriksen said. He drew a Skorpion machine pistol from within his jacket, a weapon he sometimes favored. Schucker didn't know and didn't care. Heinriksen was loyal and obedient, and that was why Schucker valued him.

There was a scuffle, followed by the sound of someone being punched in the stomach. Schucker grimaced as the man who'd been punched began to retch. The sound echoed through the parking garage. Finally, the security operatives dragged a figure from the darkness.

"Ziegler?" Schucker asked. "What in hell are you doing here?"

"You know this man, sir?" Heinriksen asked, confused.

"Yes," Schucker said. "Search him."

Heinriksen patted Ziegler down and tossed the man's personal effects on the pavement before Schucker's feet. There was a billfold, some keys and a very expensive wireless phone. Finally, Heinriksen found the identification wallet.

"Interpol!" Heinriksen said, beginning to raise the Skorpion.

"A moment, please, Gunnar," Schucker waved him off. "And do stop it. Your agitation does nothing for my mood. This is our spy within Interpol. Tell me, spy—" he directed the question to Ziegler "—would you care to tell me why you are not, at this moment, *within* Interpol?"

Ziegler floundered. "Sir, I was, I mean to say I was simply returning to report, that is…"

"Come now," Schucker said with contempt. "You can manage better than that."

Heinriksen flipped open the double agent's wireless phone and began thumbing through menus.

"You see, sir, Dumar and his people, they are, I mean, as a group they are…" Ziegler began again.

"Sir," Heinriksen said, "look at this." He held out the open phone. There was a text message: Follow David Schucker. I have my suspicions. It was signed D/E.

"Yes," Schucker said, disgusted. "I had figured that much out, Gunnar."

"Sir?"

"Isn't it obvious?" Schucker said. "This little fool is the reason Dumar and his amateurs have been one step ahead of us. Somehow he's been co-opted by more than the money we offered him to turn informant for us. Isn't that right, Ziegler?"

Ziegler looked at him but didn't say anything.

"*Now* you are silent?" Schucker said. "You've certainly done your share of talking until now. Tell me, Ziegler, is there anyone or anything you will not betray?"

"I am loyal to Iron Thunder!" Ziegler said suddenly. "Dumar Eon has shown me the way! You, all you care for is money. Interpol is a joke. The international law-enforcement community... Law enforcement for what? All of you are worms! There is only one truth, one reality, and that is the reality and the finality of death!"

"Gunnar," Schucker said, "shut him up."

Heinriksen dropped the phone on the pavement and threw a vicious straight punch into Ziegler's stomach. The agent bent double again, dry-heaving.

Schucker sighed. "That is revolting. Hit him in the head next time."

"Yes, sir," Heinriksen said.

"No, wait." Schucker held up a hand. "I'm sorry, Gunnar. I've been wasting your time. You are a loyal man and you deserve better."

"Sir?"

"Shoot him."

Heinriksen nodded. He brought up the Skorpion. The men holding Ziegler backed off several paces. Heinriksen put the stubby barrel of the crude little weapon to Ziegler's forehead. The man managed to recover sufficiently to look up defiantly, but when he saw the looming muzzle of the machine pistol, he paled.

"That final rest Dumar and your fellow maniacs are always going on about?" Schucker said. "I'm giving it to you, Ziegler. And for the miserable job you've done, I'm going to have your family killed, too."

Ziegler opened his mouth to scream in protest.

Heinriksen shot him.

Schucker was turning away before the body had finished hitting the pavement. "See to it," he said.

"Sir?" Heinriksen asked.

"The family. I wasn't kidding. I'm in a very bad mood, Gunnar, and I intend to make certain that mistakes like this do not happen in the future. I was an idiot to think someone we'd turned could not be turned again."

"Yes, sir. I mean, no, sir, you're not a fool. But I will see to it, sir."

"Good man, Gunnar," Schucker said, staring into the depths of the parking garage. "Let's get out of here before the police forget I've bribed them to stay away." Followed by his contingent of security operatives, he climbed into his car and removed his own phone from his jacket. He flipped the unit open and dialed a number from memory.

"Sir," came the reply.

"Niclas," Schucker said into his phone. "I assume you and your teams are in place?"

"Yes, sir," Niclas, another of Schucker's field men, answered. "We await your orders."

"I am accelerating the timetable. Do not wait," Schucker said. "Hit them now. Make them pay. It's time we removed this cancer. I am sick to death of these idiots."

"Yes, sir, of course, sir. Uh, sir?"

"What?"

"Sir, the munitions with which you equipped us. Do you really believe we may use them?"

"Yes!" Schucker yelled. "Use them! Spare nothing! I don't care what you have to do. I don't care who I have to pay off. I will have these damned Iron Thunder fools out from underfoot now. We'll spread enough money around after to make it work. Once word gets out that dangerous, armed cult members were entrenched in a Berlin apartment building, no one will question the methods used to remove them. We can cover up the rest. In this, we can take a cue from the Americans."

"Sir?"

"A terrorist group in an American city some years ago, Niclas," Schucker said. "So dug in were they that the authorities chose to drop a sizable bomb on them. This is no different. Clear them all. We will deal with the consequences later."

"Understood, sir."

12

"Yes, Bear has Akira going through the specifications of the phone now," Barbara Price said to Bolan over the soldier's secure wireless cell, "which were transmitted to us after you had the courier run the device to the drop house. They did a thorough job in only a little time. Akira thinks there may be a way to reverse-engineer this so we can use the phones to track Iron Thunder's members. If we can do that, we can have them picked up."

"On what grounds?" Bolan asked, curious.

"Conspiracy to commit terrorist acts, officially," Price said. "A recording of Dumar Eon's speech, minus his discussion with you, has already hit the file- and video-sharing Web sites. It's pretty obvious Iron Thunder is working itself up to something. We just don't know what yet."

"What's Hal got to say about that?" Bolan said. "Officially, he was hoping to get the powers that be on the same page, to avoid diplomatic troubles."

"He hasn't commented," Price replied, "but you know how that goes. I'd say we're pretty far into this now. I imagine preventing loss of life takes precedence over procedural wrangling."

"I agree," Bolan said. "I need a next step. What can your analysis provide, based on everything that's happened? I have to believe our priority list is shot to hell."

"Yes," Price said, "but we have a new target for you. Bear has had the team working overtime, cracking the accounts used to post and trade Iron Thunder videos, not to mention Internet discussion board accounts used to post messages sympathetic to the cult. It took some time, for obvious reasons, but of course even the most anonymous Internet post isn't as untraceable as the user thinks. After cracking account after account and cross-referencing what available data could be had for the names and addresses associated with the Internet service providers' customers—" Price paused to inhale "—Bear says he's got a curious anomaly. There's a block of flats right there in Berlin that appear to be occupied solely by Iron Thunder members."

"A clubhouse?" Bolan asked.

"You could call it that," Price said. "The best way to hide is in plain sight, and it helps if all your neighbors share your passion for murder."

"How hard a target will it be?"

"Possibly very," Price said. "We've traced the ownership records as well as leasing agreements and other public data. The Consortium owns a company that owns a company that holds the property, and Iron Thunder's people have slowly been renting units and displacing former residents for what looks like a couple of years. There's no telling what sort of complex they've got inside."

"Understood," Bolan said. "Give me the address."

"Transmitting files to your phone now."

Bolan reviewed the files, which consisted of address information, some layout on the building that may have changed since the plans were drawn up—and probably had—and exterior photographs. He toweled his hair dry and donned a fresh blacksuit. He had ordered Rieck to go to a safe location to recover and regroup, and had taken the opportunity to move to a different hotel and do the same. He had ordered a little room service and spent some time reviewing his mission data while silently refueling. He had then cleaned and reloaded his weapons, and now he replaced them in their holsters under his drover coat. It had been a long day, and would be longer. He was ready. Nighttime Berlin awaited him. He glanced at his heavy-duty stainless-steel watch, once again on his wrist. Rieck would be out front again by now. Bolan had let him borrow the BMW.

True to his word, the Interpol agent was waiting at the curb. He had a new aura of ready action. His hand was inside his coat, no doubt resting on the little H&K submachine gun. Bolan climbed into the car and nodded to him.

"Cooper," Rieck said.

"Rieck. Feeling better?"

"My head hurts, and my face feels like it's been stomped into a puddle. Oh, and I am told I have a cracked rib. But I'll live."

"Good," Bolan said. "Ready for more?"

"Very," Rieck said. He smiled grimly through his split lip. Bolan didn't blame him. After being captured, threatened and beaten, any man would be looking to inflict a little payback on his enemies. Bolan was long past that, given his experience, but there was no harm in Rieck's emotions unless he let them get the better of him. From what the soldier had seen of his Interpol liaison, the man's head was on straight and he had his fair share of psychological fortitude. Bolan didn't think there would be a problem.

Bolan gave him the address. "My people have identified a nest of Iron Thunder members," he explained. "The entire place is owned by the Consortium. They may be dug in deep. It's our best link to their membership here in Berlin, apart from the Consortium itself, and right now I'm more interested in Iron Thunder than in the company that finances it. The Consortium's offices can wait, but I don't think this can."

"All right," Rieck said. He pulled away from the curb and put his foot to the pedal, taking them briskly through Berlin. It had started raining heavily again. The pavement reflected the BMW's headlights. The city, alive with the night, blinked and flashed and glowed in all its incandescent, neon and digital glory. The rain turned the highways into molten rivers of color. Bolan watched intently as the streets passed by, committing as much of the German metropolis as possible to his memory.

"All right, let's review. Our objective," he said, "is to locate those missing chemical weapons. The cult has them, and got them through the Consortium."

"And it seems pretty likely they'll be used for whatever big event Dumar Eon is planning," Rieck said.

"Right." Bolan nodded. "But for some reason the weapons have been taken or moved, and the group of Iron Thunder members we encountered wasn't told of it. That means either they're even more disorganized than they seem, at times, or there's trouble between Iron Thunder and the Consortium's security force."

"You think Ziegler was telling the truth about that?"

"The most convincing way to lie," Bolan said, "is to use the truth most of the time. I'm willing to bet he told us more or less what he knew. He just left out that critical part about the phones, and probably warned Eon that we were on the way over once we left. We probably won't ever know if he was loyal to Iron Thunder all along, a mole planted within Interpol, or if he was turned by them."

"You think Eon and his cult could turn an agent to their side?"

"Stranger things have happened," Bolan said. "And who knows what could have been going on in his head before he was exposed to Dumar Eon and his minions? Human beings can crack in countless ways. Iron Thunder makes more sense than some cults I've seen, and draws a stronger following."

"It worries me that you seem to have such vast experience in these matters," Rieck said offhandedly. "You lead some kind of lifestyle, Cooper."

Bolan said nothing.

They parked a couple of blocks away from the target building, approaching it cautiously in the night. The memories of the carnage at Becker's condominium were fresh in Bolan's mind, and he knew better than to underestimate Iron Thunder's amateurs. They were ruthless, violent killers. The world they might have built inside the building was bound to be a dangerous one.

"Around back," Rieck suggested.

Bolan had already intended to do just that. He nodded. Rieck followed him as they skirted the building a block away, then moved in from the rear set of access doors. The glass panels had been spray-painted white from inside, which in itself wasn't all that unusual. It was what he would do, were his position reversed with the cultists'.

"Do we assume everyone within is hostile?" Rieck whispered.

"We can't afford to," Bolan said. "At least not right away. There could be innocents or minors inside, depending on how Iron Thunder's people do things. We'll have to take it apartment by apartment."

"I understand." Rieck pulled the MP-5 K forward on its sling and checked the magazine before chambering a round. "Ready," he said.

"Let's go," Bolan replied. He eased the door open, drawing the sound-suppressed Beretta 93-R from its custom shoulder holster. The hallway beyond was quiet. There were metal mailboxes inset on the facing walls.

They took the first flight of stairs, expecting to find a typical floor plan on the second level. Instead, they found a steel security door, monitored by a closed-circuit camera. No sooner did Bolan and Rieck get within range of the lens than an alarm began to sound somewhere within the building.

"There goes the element of surprise," Rieck wisecracked.

Bolan reached into the war bag slung over his shoulder and produced a plastic explosive charge. He planted it on the metal door, pressed the delay switch and motioned for Rieck to move back around the corner. They got behind cover within the stairwell and the charge blew, echoing through the enclosed space with bone-jarring intensity. The clatter of the heavy door hitting the floor was almost anticlimactic.

"Go!" Bolan said. He threw himself around the corner.

"Eisen-Donner!" someone shouted. The corridor was suddenly alive in bullets, as men and women—cultists all, from the shouts they roared—threw open their apartment doors and pulled the triggers of shotguns and automatic weapons. Bolan barely had time to ram open a door and take Rieck with him, spilling into a unit whose occupant had been slower on the draw. As the hailstorm of lead pocked the corridor behind them, Bolan and Rieck came face-to-face with a shotgun-wielding young man in a T-shirt and jeans. The Iron Thunder logo had been crudely stenciled in spray paint on the wall behind him.

"Die!" the cultist shouted in German.

Bolan put a single bullet in his brain.

Several cult members could be heard running down the hallway toward them. Bolan and Rieck stationed themselves at angles to either side of the doorway. One cultist, then another, then another stomped through the open door. The soldier and his Interpol ally cut down each one as they dashed in, recklessly failing to see the trap.

"Fools rush in!" Rieck said above the din of gunfire.

When the cultists stopped running blindingly through the killing chute he had improvised, the soldier knew he and his ally would have to move. If they became cornered and trapped in an enclosed space like this one, their lives would end in short order. Bolan reloaded the Beretta, holstered it and drew the Desert Eagle, knowing its powerful .44 Magnum rounds would be necessary for what he planned.

"Get ready," he said to Rieck. "On three, I go. Follow me. Diagonals across the hallway, from apartment to apartment, charging the gunners. On me."

"Understood!" Rieck nodded.

"One," Bolan said. "Two…three!" He charged.

Sloppy, unaimed gunfire followed him, but it didn't get close enough to be a real danger. Several cultists were firing from within their apartments by pushing their guns out the open doorways, not looking at what they were shooting, counting on the walls for cover and concealment. Bolan, however, could see that the divisions in these units were of relatively lightweight drywall, erected after the fact. The exterior shell of the building was heavy brick and mortar, but these dividers were little more than plasterboard and, presumably, insulation.

Bolan hit the next apartment on a diagonal angle from the first one. The cultist inside was hiding behind the door. He tumbled when Bolan bulled through the doorway, knocking him to the floor. Bolan put a .44 Magnum slug through his chest, turned and fired twice through the opposite wall at a forty-five-degree angle. The cultist hiding in that unit screamed, stumbled and fell, sprawling halfway into the hall.

The gunfire intensified as Bolan threw himself into the next doorway, leaping over the corpse. The cultists had realized what was happening and were determined not to fall prey to the same tactics. The Executioner was ready for that, reaching into his war bag to produce several flash-bang grenades.

Rieck joined him. Bolan, gun pointed to the floor, motioned with the flash-bang in his other hand and mouthed "grenade." The Interpol agent nodded, hunching his shoulders as if to cover his ears. Bolan nodded back.

A fresh wave of gunfire rolled through the space between them. The cultists were still firing blind but were emptying their guns as fast as they could load them, trying to erect a wall of flying bullets between themselves and the invaders. Bolan waited for the fusillade to abate somewhat, indicating that at least a couple of cultists were reloading. Then he started to activate flash-bangs, and toss them down the hallway, bouncing them off open doorways, as if playing a dangerous game of explosive billiards. The lethal little metal eggs caromed and rolled and found their way down the corridor and into several apartments.

Bolan pressed his arms against his ears, squeezed his eyes shut and turned away. The flash-bangs burst, one after another. The blinding white flashes and deafening explosions were followed by overlapping screams as the weapons did their terrible work. Bolan, guns in hand, wasted no time. He sprinted down the hallway, blasting writhing cultists as he passed their open doorways. It was brutal work, but there was no other way. This nest of killers couldn't be allowed to leave, couldn't be permitted to unleash Iron Thunder's evil on the people of Berlin and of the world.

Bolan encountered another metal security door at the opposite end of the building. Rather than blow it, he backtracked. He met Rieck halfway, and the two men checked each apartment for survivors. There were two men who appeared to have shot themselves with their own weapons, but the rest had fallen to the Executioner's guns. There were no cultists left alive.

"Good God, Cooper," Rieck said. Bolan changed the magazines in his pistols, then holstered the Beretta. With the Desert Eagle in his fist, he looked down the corridor ahead.

"There's another door," he said, "and at least one more level above. Likely there will be more of them up there. Ready to do this again?"

"No," Rieck said, shaking his head and reloading the MP-5 K, "but I don't think we have a choice."

"None at all."

"Then let's do it."

They took a step toward the door. Bolan reached into his war bag for another charge.

The building rumbled beneath them.

Bolan, realizing what was happening, grabbed Rieck and threw both of them into the nearest open doorway. The explosion that filled the corridor again shook the building. Outside, some mighty force was hammering the structure. The smoke, debris and brick dust in the hallway was testament to its power.

"What was that?" Rieck asked.

"Rocket-propelled grenade, I think," Bolan said. He risked a peek out the doorway.

"They're shooting at us from upstairs?" Rieck asked.

"Not upstairs," Bolan said. "Out there."

Rieck couldn't help himself; he took a look around the corner of the doorway. The hole in the side of the building was still smoking, and the carnage in the corridor was unspeakable. Rubble and mangled bodies were everywhere. Through the gaping wound in the brick shell, Bolan and Rieck could see well-dressed men running around a group of dark sedans parked below.

More gunfire sounded, but this time it was directed outside. The cultists on the next level were firing at the men there.

"The Consortium's security operatives," Rieck stated. "It has to be."

"Probably," Bolan agreed. "We're caught in the middle."

"Well, that's not the only problem," Rieck said. "While they're fighting each other we have no one to root for."

Bolan didn't comment. He checked his weapons. "New plan," he said. "Get to the rear of this apartment. We're going back out the way we came."

"We're going to meet our new friends on the way out?"

"Better than waiting for them to find us here and close us in." Bolan nodded. "Come on."

They ran for it.

13

The men working their way up the stairwell were heavily armed with assault rifles, grenade launchers and the RPG. Bolan met the first of them charging up, and the last thing they expected was the juggernaut that came at them from above. As he rounded the corner at the top of the stairwell, he planted one combat boot in the chest of the lead man, knocking the group sprawling. He began pumping 3-round bursts from the Beretta 93-R into the cluster of shooters, emptying the 20-round magazine.

It was a rout.

Bolan, with Rieck and his MP-5 K backing him up, pushed the enemy back down the stairs, the shooters tumbling over one another. Rieck shot the man with the RPG launcher, and Bolan jumped over the body as he continued blitzing his way downward.

"Grab that!" he shouted to Rieck, pointing to the launcher.

They hit ground level and the exit doors. Rieck threw open the door…and immediately backed up.

"Look out!" he shouted.

The armored vehicle was a large, four-wheeled armored personnel carrier of the type used by SWAT and other special tactics units. This one bore no markings, but if these were indeed Consortium security personnel, it probably was among the resources on which they could call. There was no weapon mounted on the APC, but it was blocking the doorway. A gun port faced down the hall. As Bolan and Rieck backed toward the corner of the stairwell leading up, that port slid open and the muzzle of a machine gun poked out.

"Go, go, go," Bolan urged.

Bullets from the heavy machine gun tore through the hallway, sending debris flying. The soldier and his Interpol ally raced back up the stairs. If they couldn't go down, their only option was up…and out.

Gunfire continued from the upper level as the Iron Thunder cultists shot down at the gunners in the street. Bolan hoped this would provide sufficient distraction while he and Rieck made their way into Iron Thunder's midst.

Bolan palmed his last grenade from his war bag as they ran. They hit the next level and then the facing stairwell. The soldier motioned for Rieck to cover the hall behind them, then he popped the pin on the grenade, counted down the numbers and threw the explosive metal egg up the stairs.

The explosion rattled the building and drew dust from the ceiling panels overhead. Bolan filled his hands with hardware, the Desert Eagle in his right and the Beretta 93-R in his left. He sprayed the charred doorway space with bullets. It was a risky play, but it was also the only option.

The Executioner burst through the doorway, kicking the steel security door aside on its mangled hinges. The floor plan of this level was open, a recreation room of sorts; he noted in an eyeblink the layout of tables, sofas and a kitchenette area. A shattered large-screen television was mounted to one bullet-pocked wall, which bore the Iron Thunder logo in spray paint.

A cultist with a revolver drew down on him from the cover of an overturned couch. Bolan put a .44 Magnum slug through the gunman's temple.

Gunfire converged from three separate points. Bolan threw himself forward, rolling on one shoulder, as bullets ripped the floor behind him. Then he was on his feet again, turning and engaging the enemy, the Beretta 93-R spitting 3-round bursts and the Desert Eagle booming. First one, then a second, then a third cultist fell and died. Bolan hit the bloodied floor again, his chin in a pile of hot shell casings. Several shots came from outside, angled high through the shattered windows.

Then it was quiet.

"Rieck!" Bolan called. "It's clear! Get up here!"

The Interpol agent hustled up the stairwell. He ducked into the recreation level and surveyed the scene; then he pushed the metal door back in place and dragged a heavy, battle-scarred lounge chair into position to block it.

"Over there." Bolan motioned with his left arm, crabbing his way toward the nearest set of broken windows. He pointed to the kitchenette, from which Rieck would have a good line of fire to the door, while taking advantage of the natural cover of the angle. "Watch that entry. They'll send men back up the stairs when they realize what's happened."

"Got it," Rieck said. He looked around at the bodies on the floor. Bolan nodded grimly. They were surrounded by corpses, some shot from below by the professionals in the street, and some killed under Bolan's guns.

"Why aren't they shooting?" Rieck asked as he took his position.

"They're not stupid," Bolan said. "They're fully aware there's no one left inside shooting at them. Right now they're trying to figure out what happened to the team sent to take the stairs. When they figure it out, they'll mount another assault."

"So what do we do?" Rieck asked. "We can't just wait here to get shot."

"I don't intend to," Bolan said. He found what he'd come for. One of the dead cultists by the wall had met his final bliss clutching a Steyr Scout rifle. Bolan pried the weapon from the dead man's hands, worked the bolt and found the 5-round box magazine empty. He found three spares on the body and rammed one home, working the bolt again to chamber the round.

The Leupold M-8 scope was only two and a half power, but it would be sufficient for the short range. For Bolan, a trained and experienced sniper, the rifle was a surgeon's scalpel. He brought the weapon to his shoulder, positioned himself in a corner of the window and surveyed the scene outside as he took aim.

The APC was parked directly below, blocking the doors into the building. Some distance from that, a line of Mercedes sedans formed a barrier, behind which the shooters were arrayed. A few of them were looking up at the building, but Bolan's silhouette was minimal enough that they didn't notice him immediately.

Bolan lined up a shot through the window of one of the sedans. The shooters below were sloppy or complacent; they were crouched behind the cars but not behind the engine blocks, which were the only portion of the vehicles that afforded real protection from serious small arms. One of the men was leaning over the roof of the car, bracing a handgun pointed up toward the building.

Bolan put a .308 Winchester round through his heart. The 7.62 mm NATO round drilled the man and spun him. He collapsed to the ground without a sound.

The crack of the rifle alerted the others. They began to shoot at the building blindly, unsure of the sniper's exact location. Bolan worked the bolt, tracked left and took a second man through the head when the target poked out from behind the trunk of one of the cars. The Executioner followed that up with two rapid shots. The shooters below panicked and emptied their guns into the building. When the bullets came close to his location, Bolan ducked back and rode it out. The thick exterior walls stopped any rounds that might otherwise have been a danger to him.

"We've got movement on the stairwell!"

Bolan turned and pressed his back to the wall. He put the Steyr on the floor and pulled the Beretta 93-R, making sure it was set to 3-round burst. The noise beyond the door was picking up; there were shouts and the sound of shoes on the stairs beyond.

"Down!" Bolan ordered. He covered his head with one arm and Rieck ducked behind the kitchenette counter.

Predictably, the explosive charge detonated. It was what Bolan would have done, and he was ready for it. When the door blew inward, pushing the lounge chair aside, he thrust the Beretta forward and started to fire into the cloud of smoke and flame. An instant later, the chatter of Rieck's deadly submachine gun joined the barks of the suppressed Beretta.

The killers were torn apart as they charged the door, wrongly thinking that they held the initiative in their direct assault. Bolan mowed them down and Rieck mopped them up, their guns playing a deadly 9 mm duet. When the Beretta coughed and went silent, its 20-round magazine expended, Bolan switched to the Desert Eagle. His .44 Magnum rounds were like lightning bolts thrown by an avenging god, striking down the last of the invading gunners.

There was a pause. Bolan took the opportunity to reload his weapons, wielding both guns as he moved from his position and advanced on the bullet-riddled doorway. Rieck did the same.

"It's clear!" Rieck shouted loudly. His ears were probably ringing very badly. Bolan's own had suffered under the onslaught, but he was more accustomed to it. It was actually nothing short of a miracle that the veteran soldier didn't suffer from permanent hearing loss, but Mack Bolan had long ago written that off to luck, good genes, or both.

A smoke detector was wailing somewhere in the building. That was ironic, to Bolan's thinking. A group of people whose twisted religion was devoted to the glorification of death still had a smoke detector in place where they lived. He ignored the noise. Rieck started checking bodies, nudging them with his toe as he covered them with the H&K.

Bolan holstered the Desert Eagle and, with the Beretta in his right hand, began doing the same. The building was a charnel house. Countless bullet holes peppered the walls. Bodies were everywhere, in some places two and three deep. The carpets were soaked in blood. Several small fires burned. Bolan went to the devastated kitchenette, where the worst of the fires was beginning to blaze, and ripped a small fire extinguisher from its bracket on the wall. By sheer luck it hadn't been pierced by a bullet. He sprayed out the flames, found another one across the recreation level and emptied the extinguisher. He tossed the empty canister aside, again thinking of the irony that such a precaution was in place here.

"Cooper!" Rieck called. "I've got a live one. No, two!"

The Executioner went to stand next to Rieck, who held his weapon on two wounded men. One was recovering from a graze to the scalp that had knocked him sprawling. The other had a badly mangled leg and had also taken a round through one arm, which was hanging limply. Both men were now sitting on the floor, leaning against the wall to the left of the smoking doorway.

"Either of them speak English?" Bolan asked.

"This one does." Rieck nodded to the one with the head graze. "The other man does not."

Bolan searched both men as Rieck stood guard. When he was satisfied that neither gunner had a hidden weapon and that there was nothing within reach that could be used against him, he squatted to put himself at eye level with the prisoners.

"I have questions," Bolan said simply. "Will you answer them?"

"Nein." The man shook his head, his hand pressed against the bloody groove in his scalp. He sounded pained and was probably working on a pretty good concussion.

"Allow me to reiterate," Bolan said. He drew the Desert Eagle, made a show of thumbing the hammer back, and pressed the triangular snout of the massive handgun against the forehead of the other prisoner. "You will answer my questions or I will blow your friend's brains all over you, and then I will kill *you*." It was again a bluff; Bolan wasn't in the business of executing helpless prisoners. But he needed information, and he needed it as quickly as he could get it.

The prisoner wavered. His eyes went to his comrade and then back to Bolan.

"Look," Rieck said, "this isn't necessary. We're not interested in you. We're only after Iron Thunder, the very people you were fighting."

Bolan looked at him. That was not strictly true, but if it helped loosen the prisoner's tongue, it was fine with the soldier. To the prisoner, he said, "Are you willing to die for Dumar Eon? Is he worth it?"

The prisoner shook his head slowly.

"What's your name?" Rieck asked.

"Niclas," the man replied sullenly.

"Well, Niclas, that's a start," Bolan said. "Now, quickly. There's not much time. Iron Thunder was previously in possession of certain chemical weapons. They now appear not to be. Would you happen to know anything about that?"

"No," Niclas said.

"Niclas," Bolan said menacingly, "do not lie to me." He pressed the Desert Eagle more forcefully against the other prisoner's head. "If you don't care about your friend here, I can understand that. But when I'm done with him and you won't tell me anything, I won't have any reason not to shoot you, too."

"All right, all right," Niclas said, swearing in German several times. "The Syrians, the Syrians. We are selling the weapons to the Syrians."

"What Syrians would those be?" Bolan asked.

"I don't know!" Niclas shook his head and then regretted the gesture. He groaned and pressed his fist more tightly against the furrow there. "Syrians, that is all I was told! The meet was today. It is probably already done."

"Where was the meet?"

"A parking garage," Niclas said. He rattled off an address.

Bolan gestured with the pistol, sensing the man was holding back. "All right!" he said again. "The Syrians have been given use of one of our safehouses. They will stage the weapons there until they can be moved." He gave up the address.

"What's their timetable?" Bolan pressed.

"I don't know." Niclas groaned miserably. "We aren't told such things."

"Confirm for me," Bolan said, "just who 'we' is."

"Sicherheit Vereinigung," Niclas said. "I am security."

"These other men? You're mercenaries, aren't you?"

"Some of us," Niclas admitted.

"And the reason you were shooting Iron Thunder members? You're all supposed to be on the same side."

Niclas spit and then held his skull again. "Those madmen?" he said, incredulous. "We were *never* on their side. It was a pleasure finally to bring death to them, as they so often said they wished. Crazy, all of them! Sadists and madmen, claiming they valued only death. Long have we tolerated their interference and cleaned up after their ill-considered games."

"Who do you answer to?" Bolan asked.

Niclas looked at the floor. He was caught, and he knew it. Bolan imagined that, as he truly weighed his loyalties, he was finding little reason not to roll over on those who had sent him to do their dirty work.

"My men and I take our orders from David Schucker," Niclas said finally. "He is head of—"

"Operations for the Security Consortium," Rieck supplied. "I *knew* it."

"Rieck," Bolan said, "get the authorities on the phone. This place is a war zone. It should be crawling with cops, government officials, military, something. Where is everybody?"

"Bought off?" Rieck speculated.

"Looks like," Bolan nodded. "Shake their tree. They can't ignore what's going on here forever. Get them out here. We need this crime scene controlled. I'll need you to keep an eye on things and run interference."

"You're going to this safehouse?"

"Yes," Bolan said. "I've got to move fast. We need to stop those chemicals before they leave the country, or else we'll never get our hands on them. You can handle these two?"

"Yes, of course," Rieck said. "I will be fine. Cooper?"

"Yeah?"

"Try not to get shot. I've been enjoying our work together." He grinned through his split lip, and the bruises on his face made him wince.

"Yeah, I can tell," Bolan said. "You *look* like you're having fun."

14

Half an hour later, Bolan parked the BMW between two smaller cars on a narrow side street. Under cover of night, he made sure his war bag was slung across his body and that his weapons were fully loaded. He dropped his drover coat on the backseat of the car. Rigged for battle, he walked down the block and circled the safehouse address.

It was a small, historic building squeezed between two larger edifices, in a mixed neighborhood that appeared partly residential and partly commercial. Even in a city as busy as Berlin, at this hour the area was relatively quiet. Bolan crept along the row of buildings, moving silently, a wraith on a mission of justice.

When he saw the figure walking the sidewalk in front of the target building, he knew the man for what he was: a sentry.

Dressed in a leather bomber jacket, jeans and boots, the big man was doing a good job of trying to look casual. Bolan, concealed in the shadow of a neighboring building, watched him for a few minutes. He kept walking the same path back and forth in front of the safehouse. There was a streetlamp not far away, and Bolan marked the sentry's passage by the number of times he crossed the circle of light. Periodically the guard touched his jacket just forward of his left hip. That was the sign of a man carrying a gun who was nervous, agitated or simply uncomfortable. It was the act of a man reassuring himself that the piece was there, that it hadn't shifted or fallen.

Bolan watched for twenty minutes more, listening to the numbers fall in his head. When he was satisfied that the sentry was alone and not being watched by someone inside the safehouse, he made his move. He simply emerged from the shadows and walked casually down the street, heading toward him.

The man started at Bolan's sudden appearance. The soldier, his eyes locked on the end of the street, passed right by the sentry, nodding cheerfully as both men occupied the circle of illumination. He paused as if suddenly remembering something, turned back and made a show of patting down his pockets.

"Say," he said quietly, "you wouldn't have a cigarette, would you?"

When the sentry stared at him, confused, Bolan asked again, more slowly. He pantomimed smoking a cigarette and again repeated his request, playing the Ugly American to the hilt.

The sentry was suspicious but didn't dare draw attention to the safehouse by being rude. He produced a cigarette from a pack taken from his jacket pocket. He held this out to Bolan.

The soldier reached with his left hand to take the cigarette—and grabbed the sentry by the wrist. He pulled with all his might, yanking the man off balance and straight into Bolan's rock-hard right fist. Something in the sentry's face crunched. He opened his mouth to shout and Bolan hammered him again. The sentry went limp and dropped to the sidewalk.

The Executioner held his breath. The neighborhood remained quiet, except for the low thrum of the city itself. Satisfied, Bolan dragged the man into the shadows of the alleyway between the buildings. The gun the man carried in a cross-draw holster was a 1911-type .45. Bolan took it, unloaded it and stripped the slide away. He dumped the components and then secured the unconscious sentry with plastic zip-tie cuffs. Finally, he used duct tape from his war bag to gag and blindfold him.

Moving quickly and silently, he crept to the front of the safehouse, walked up the stone steps and risked peering through one of the curtained windows facing the street. Lights burned inside. Satisfied, Bolan went back the way he came, stepped over the prone figure in the alley and went around to the rear. He found a heavy wooden door and another window. The window was shuttered, but he could tell that here, too, lights were on inside. Moving up to the door, he put his ear to the wood. The voices inside were speaking in Arabic, which he recognized easily.

Another, louder voice suddenly spoke up. The Arabic conversation ceased. This new voice was in accented English, and had the tone of a man speaking on a phone over a bad connection.

"It is Assan," the voice said. "Assan Bashir!" There was cursing in Arabic. "Can you hear me or can you not? What? Wait… Yes, that is better. Yes. I said, it is Assan. I want you to pass on word to my father. Yes! What?… Then get a pen and write it down, you fool! Do as I tell you." As Bashir waited impatiently—at least, Bolan pictured him doing so—he paced back and forth. Bolan watched the shadows play across the curtained window.

"What?" Bashir responded again. "Yes, the scrambler is in place. Yes. Do not worry! All is ready. The cargo is here, with me. I am arranging for its transport. Tell father I will have it shipped and be on the same plane back. Yes. Tomorrow morning. Yes. Yes, I said! Very well." The loud sigh of exasperation was audible even through the door. Bashir began hissing rapidly in Arabic, uttering what Bolan could only assume was profanity. The man's tone changed as he raised his voice; now it was that of a man in charge addressing subordinates. He was, Bolan thought, probably verifying the plans to ship the "cargo"—what could only be the chemical weapons—in the morning.

Of course, he could simply be ordering dinner, too, but the implications of the phone call remained. Some means of transportation Bashir had arranged would be waiting, most likely to take the weapons to Syria. While Bashir himself wouldn't be making the rendezvous, Bolan would have to recount his phone call to the Farm. Whatever power play the Bashir family was contemplating, something involving nerve gas and other chemical weapons would be of interest to Stony Man's data analysts. It was just the sort of advance tip that might prompt another mission to head off the problem.

There was, Bolan thought, a time and a place for such business. For now, he had more immediate work to do.

With the suppressed Beretta 93-R in hand, the Executioner stepped to the side of the door. He tapped on it faintly, then he tapped again. An angry voice from inside spoke in Arabic. When Bolan tapped a third time, he heard the door latch being pulled back. The angry face that appeared as the door was thrown open froze in shock as the barrel of the Beretta came up.

Bolan put a finger to his lips. "Shh," he said.

The man shouted in Arabic and grabbed for the gun in his shoulder holster.

The Executioner shot him.

Bolan put a single round between the man's eyes. The body fell to the kitchen floor. This room in the back of the safehouse was dominated by a round kitchen table, a bright ceiling lamp and a dusty metal stove that looked to be an antique. Bolan was already turning to engage his second target as he took in these details. Like the first armed man, this second gunman wore a business suit. He was going for an Uzi that sat on the kitchen table. Bolan drilled him through the neck with a single 9 mm round, then flipped the Beretta 93-R to 3-round burst.

Never one to waste a tactic that worked, Bolan fished a flash-bang grenade from his war bag, pulled the pin and counted down as the spoon spun away. He threw the grenade against the wall next to the open doorway leading from the kitchen. The flash-bang bounced and ricocheted into the next room. The soldier covered his ears, closed his eyes tightly and opened his mouth. The deafening blast was painfully bright even through his eyelids.

The men in the next room were screaming. Bolan crouched and glided through the doorway, both hands clutching the Beretta. He took careful aim and drilled each writhing gunman through the head or chest.

As quickly as the firefight had started, it was over. The sudden silence roared in the Executioner's ears.

Gun up and probing, he surveyed the bodies arrayed before him. Any of them could be Bashir, but he didn't think so. They were dressed relatively plainly and, more importantly, almost identically. Some were wearing jackets and some were not, but they were like cookie-cutter copies of each other; these men would be Bashir's security detail.

The ceiling above him creaked, just once.

That answered that. Bashir and possibly more men would be waiting upstairs for their attacker to come calling. The soldier could expect to walk into a bullet, or many of them, as soon as he reached the landing at the top of the stairs.

He waited.

It was a gamble, of course; there was a chance the police would show up in response to the disturbance, unless the Consortium had somehow paid for discretion in relation to what went on at their safehouse. Bolan was betting he wouldn't have to wait long for the enemy to appear.

He stationed himself behind the doorway to the kitchen, where he had just enough view of the stairs leading to the second floor. Sure enough, in a few minutes a pair of shoes appeared. Bolan watched but made no move. Eventually the man on the stairs—another bodyguard, from the look of him—was fully visible, the heavy Magnum revolver in his hands held before him like a magic wand. He was a very large man, with almost no neck to speak of. His shoulders strained the suit he wore. He looked nervous, and for good reason. Several of his fellows had just been killed in an eyeblink.

Bolan waited for the man to turn away, frantically looking in every direction at once. When the angle was best, the soldier said, "Don't move."

The bodyguard swung the barrel of the revolver toward Bolan with a cry of alarm. The Executioner shot him. The 3-round burst took the man in the heart, but he was charging forward like an enraged rhino. Perhaps already dead on his feet, the bodyguard crashed into Bolan and took him to the floor, his fingers locked in a death grip around his throat. The Beretta was knocked from his grasp as he hit the floor with rib-cracking force, three hundred pounds of near deadweight on top of him.

Bolan tried to push off the dying man. He could feel the Desert Eagle being clawed from its holster, but there was nothing he could do about it. His own hands were the only thing keeping the fingers around his throat from strangling the life out of him.

Silently, the two men fought. Finally, the messages from his body caught up with the big bodyguard's brain. His fingers went limp and he slumped on top of the soldier, the death rattle low in his throat leaving no doubt of his passing. Bolan rolled the corpse off himself.

And looked up into the barrel of a Browning Hi-Power.

On instinct, Bolan slapped the gun away. It spun across the room, and the man before him—a squat, ugly man with gold rings on his fingers—smiled viciously.

He yanked a *kindjal* from his waistband. The curved, wickedly tapered dagger glittered in his hand. "You take my gun," he said, "and I simply stab you with my knife."

"Bashir," Bolan said.

Bolan's apparent recognition of the Syrian surprised him. It was enough of a distraction. The big American lashed out with a combat-booted foot, catching Bashir in the thigh, sending him reeling. The Executioner drew the double-edged Sting dagger from his waistband and held it low against his body, his free hand up and ready, the knife between him and his opponent.

"I will kill you!" Bashir growled. "I will dance on your corpse. I will find your family and I will have them killed. I—" The Syrian launched his attack in midsentence, hoping to fool his opponent with the sudden move.

Bolan was ready for it; he slipped back and slashed Bashir as he went past. The squat man shrieked and whirled, slashing at the air repeatedly, trying to drive Bolan away. The soldier waited, letting the Syrian waste his energy, biding time until a serious strike came.

"You have no words, dog?" Bashir said. "Can you not understand me?" He switched to Arabic, and then to what was probably horribly accented and broken German. Bolan gave him nothing. Bashir, growing more and more agitated, charged again, this time with a clumsy overhead attack that became a much deadlier backhand thrust as the man stabbed at Bolan. The Executioner slapped and blocked, passing Bashir's knife hand, and thrust out with a brutal, pistoning side kick to Bashir's knee. The Syrian screamed as something gave and he collapsed onto the floor.

Bolan kicked the knife away. Watching Bashir the entire time, he retrieved his guns, wiped clean and sheathed his knife, then stood over Bashir with the Desert Eagle drawn.

"The nerve gas," Bolan said.

"American!" Bashir said, confused. "But why? How?"

"Does it matter?" Bolan said. "The nerve gas." He thumbed back the hammer of the weapon."

"Upstairs," Bashir said, gritting his teeth against the pain in his knee. He was bleeding freely from the slash on his arm, but the wound wasn't that serious. "It is all upstairs."

"Then we're done here," Bolan said.

"Wait, American," Bashir said. "You like money, yes? I have much money. Let me go, allow me to leave, and I will see that you are richly rewarded."

"I don't think so," Bolan said. He watched Bashir intently, prepared for any sudden move.

"A million dollars," Bashir said. "Perhaps in euros? Name your price, American."

"Some things," Bolan said, "can't be bought."

"No," Bashir said. "Perhaps…not!" He whipped his wrist upward, and a small pocket automatic pistol fell from his sleeve onto the carpet. Before he could scoop it up, Bolan put a .44 Magnum slug through the terrorist's brain.

The shot echoed through the room.

Bolan bent and picked up the small .25-caliber pistol. A search of Bashir's body revealed a thick wad of euros in a money clip, an expensive satellite phone and the leather holster on his forearm. Not quite a superspy gadget, and not all that practical, but still cunning and dangerous.

He took the steps upstairs cautiously, mindful of hidden enemies. There were no other men alive in the stone-fronted dwelling. He found two rooms upstairs, each full of canisters and crates. The nerve gas and assorted other nasty chemical weapons were there, all right. Bolan pulled out his secure phone.

"Price," Stony Man's mission controller answered in due course.

"Striker," Bolan said. "Tell Hal I have some good news. I'm standing in a room full of chemical weapons."

"That's good news?" Aaron "the Bear" Kurtzman's voice joined the call.

"It is now," Bolan said, "because I need you to send a team we can trust to package them up and get them out of here." He recited the address.

"I have some local people we can use," Price said. "I'll get them scrambled right away. What about you?"

"Lots to do," Bolan said.

"Be careful, big guy."

"Always."

Bolan cut the connection. He took one last look around the room full of lethal cargo. A lot of very bad people had died so that he could stand in this spot.

He had a feeling there would be many more before the mission was over.

15

David Schucker sat at the head of the long, broad conference table. This room in the headquarters of the Security Consortium was among its most ostentatious. A giant plasma screen, used for Internet conferencing, dominated one wall. The high-backed rolling chairs set around the long table were among the most expensive available, each upholstered in fine leather. On the burnished table, crystal decanters of ice water waited with expensive tumblers. At each place setting, a formal written proposal waited. Each man seated at the table was a member of the board of directors of the Consortium. They met only rarely, and had never before met on such short notice. This day, however, wasn't an ordinary day.

Schucker cleared his throat. He pressed a button on the remote control before him. The lights in the conference room dimmed. The plasma screen flared to life with a prepackaged video presentation. There was no sound; the charts, graphs and text of his proposal flashed silently on the screen as Schucker stood in the darkened room.

"Ladies and gentlemen of the board," he said in German. "Good morning. I apologize for the early hour, and I thank you for meeting with me on this urgent matter. I will be brief so as to occupy as little of your precious time as possible."

There were murmurs of assent from among the board members.

"The Security Consortium," Schucker said, orating now, playing to his audience. This was one of his skills, and one of the reasons he had been so comfortable during his tenure in charge of the company's varied operations. "A vertically integrated operation that is built on acquisition. To profit, we must grow. To grow, we must expand. To expand, we must acquire. All of you are well aware of the unconventional means whereby we accomplish this as efficiently and totally as possible."

Again, there were murmurs of assent.

"Now," Schucker went on, "the time has come for certain changes in our operation. The Consortium grew, as you well know, from the investment expertise of one man. That man, known as Dumar Eon, is also the head of an organization called Iron Thunder. In its earlier days, Iron Thunder was the means through which various difficult acquisitions were facilitated. Over the years, as the Consortium has grown, and as it has grown more complex, our own professional security personnel have supplanted Iron Thunder's members."

There was some uncomfortable fidgeting among the board. They knew what he was talking about, and the subject had never been a popular one. They looked the other way because the Consortium had made them—or kept them—wealthy. The board members didn't like confronting the issue directly.

"The simple fact," Schucker said, "is that Iron Thunder has become a distinct liability. Though once tolerated, it can no longer be allowed to continue operating as part of this organization. We must divorce ourselves from Dumar Eon and his group. We have no choice."

"But," one of the board members said, "Dumar Eon owns this company."

"No," Schucker said, "he does not. No one man owns the Consortium, in fact. It is specifically designed to operate independently of any one man, or of any ten men. Or women," he added. "The fact is, the Consortium has continued as smoothly as it has because I have seen to its mechanics. You know me. You know my record. You know that I am reliable. I am no wild-eyed ideologue—" Schucker gestured toward himself before spreading his hands to take in the board "—and you are not mindless followers. You are businesspeople, and what I recommend is nothing more than a business proposition."

At the back of the darkened conference room, the door opened and closed. Schucker suppressed his irritation at this straggling board member's late entrance. He didn't wish to repeat his little speech, but he might have to. He needed the support of every board member he could persuade, in order to forestall any future difficulties. He was in this for the long term, after all.

"Iron Thunder and Dumar Eon are diseased limbs," Schucker said grandly, "who must be cut from the tree lest they infect the rest of us and endanger our healthy growth. I have already taken steps to see that this occurs."

"You've initiated a war, is what you've done," another board member observed.

"Yes, I'm aware of the news reports of last night's terrorist attack," Schucker said. "For that is what we are calling it—an act of terrorism by the dangerous religious cult Iron Thunder, which has no ties to any known or legitimate entity and whose operations our own security people—hired as contractors and consultants to our local law-enforcement agencies—sacrificed their lives to interdict. It's playing well and our hired help among the national news media are doing their best to keep it that way. Ladies and gentlemen, there is no need to fear."

"What, then?" asked the board member who had spoken first.

"Why, we move forward," Schucker said. "We move forward into a world marked by our Consortium's renewed dedication to business ventures that are in our best interests, with none of these schemes or crazy ideas cooked up by the old guard. I cannot promise that divesting ourselves of Dumar Eon and Iron Thunder will be quick or easy, but it is possible. I guarantee that. I will see to it. I am asking simply that you bear with me, and that you grant me your consent to proceed in the manner I see fit. To date I have taken those measures deemed necessary by me, measures within my purview as head of operations. I am asking simply that you continue to support me as the need for decisive action grows greater."

In the back of the room, the late board member began to clap slowly. "Oh," he said, "that was *stirring*. Bravo, Herr Schucker. Bravo."

"Oh, my God," Schucker said.

Dumar Eon walked deliberately to the bank of light switches and turned them on. The board members blinked at the sudden brightness. When they realized what was happening, they, too, looked stricken.

"Dumar…I…" Schucker paused.

"You have a gift for public speaking," Eon said. "Of course, I knew that. I would not have hired you otherwise. But I must admit I underestimated you."

"Dumar, please, you don't understand."

"Don't ruin it now, David," Eon said. "Please. Have some dignity." He stalked down the length of the conference table, enjoying the waves of fear that washed over him from the assembled board members. "Oh, yes," he said. "I know everything. I will admit I was a bit slow to suspect your ambitions went so far as usurping me." He laughed. "But did you really think I would not put in place certain safeguards? How many of my people did you think your security men could kill before word got back to me? Then of course there was poor Ziegler. He willingly gave himself to us, and then he was only too happy to betray both Interpol and you. Thanks to him, I knew your machinations for what they were. When you mounted your attacks last night, there was no more uncertainty. I knew you for the assassin of kings you hope to be."

"Is that what you are, Dumar?" Schucker said. "Or should I say Helmut Schribner?"

"I don't like that name," Eon said. His voice held a note of warning.

"Oh, come on, Helmut," Schucker said. He was sick and tired of the man's bravado. Did he really think he could just waltz in here and put Schucker on the defensive? David Schucker, who had so much more training, so much more knowledge, so many more resources? David Schucker, who would lead this company into the future? David Schucker, who had been planning for month after month the means, the methodology and the master plan whereby he would excise Iron Thunder and its maniacal leader? No, Schucker had had quite enough. "You're out of your league, Helmut. You're going nowhere fast. Get out of here. Get out of here while I will still allow it, or I'll have security dump your body in the river. What do you think of *that,* Helmut? I've known for *years.* Did you think you could keep any of your petty secrets from me?"

The cold rage in Dumar Eon's eyes was terrifying to behold. Schucker realized, too late, that he'd crossed over some unforgivable point of no return. "I told you not to call me that," Eon said flatly. "And I think it is time that certain things were corrected."

At some signal from Eon—perhaps he was wearing a wire to which his people were listening—the door to the conference room opened again. Several figures filed in. Schucker recognized them from the looks of utter devotion in their eyes as they gazed at Dumar Eon. These were Iron Thunder members.

Two men with H&K UMP submachine guns, possibly taken from the Consortium's own armory, took up positions at either side of the door. The cultists surrounding the conference table all held knives, of various wicked and fearsome designs.

"I cannot help but be disappointed," Eon said, "for I had thought that, while you did not share my vision, you were at least content to do your job and obey my instructions. I became suspicious when you started diverting resources to your own ends, but of course that could have been simple greed, and I can forgive greed if the greedy still serve me well." He began to pace up and down next to the conference table. The board members watched him, while the Iron Thunder cultists watched the board. Schucker could feel the tension in the room building.

"I lost many good people in your attacks last night," Eon said. "And yes, I know it was you. My people are not fools, as you seem to think. Before they died, they made certain the knowledge of your crimes was transmitted to me through countless means. I had hoped to build to a monumental message, a message worthy of Iron Thunder's greatness. You sought to deprive me of that. I have thwarted you. What remained of your forces, those you recalled to this building to protect you, is no longer. You will find not a single Consortium security operative alive in this place."

He snapped his fingers. One of the cultists, who had a backpack slung over her shoulders, pulled it off. She removed something from it and placed it on the conference table.

It was Gunnar Heinriksen's head.

"I will give you credit," Eon said. "You selected him, and he was a good man, and loyal to the end. He fought bravely, and killed many of my team as we tried to overrun him. I think he knew that, were we to get past him, you would be next. He never once begged for his life, either, not even when we were sawing his head off oh so laboriously. A brave man. Frankly, he was more worthy than the rest of these… creatures." He pointed at the board members.

"While you plied these fools with your message and corrupted them, and watched them smile and nod in their betrayal of me," Eon said, growing more angry as he spoke, "my good people and I brought the gift of oblivion to all of the personnel in this building."

It was then that Schucker realized the cultists surrounding him had blood on their hands. It was on their clothes, too. He hadn't noticed it at first, dazzled as he was by the sudden change in lighting. He realized, too, that the cloying scent he'd first thought to be his own fear was entirely too real. It was the smell of blood, of death. The cultists reeked of it.

"Wait, Dumar," he said quickly. "This is all a misunderstanding. I did what I did for the company, surely. We can work this out. We can keep building. Say the word, and I'll pass the appropriate directives down the line. We can still make this work. We can still work together."

"No," Eon said. "I don't think so. Even if I believed you, which of course I don't."

"But, Dumar," Schucker said plaintively. "After all this time? Please, we can… It doesn't have to be like this. It doesn't. Let me just make a few calls. I can make this right! I can make this right again!"

"No," Eon said.

"Dumar," Schucker said. "Look, you want me to show you that I can be devoted? I can kneel. Let me show you." He crouched, his hand drifting toward his right front pocket.

"And now, David," Eon said, stalking toward Schucker, "I am going to beat you to death."

Schucker went for the pocket automatic pistol he carried. Eon slapped it away contemptuously. He backhanded Schucker so hard that the smaller man's teeth rattled. Then he grabbed Schucker by the collar, bent him backward on the coffee table and pinned him there with one impossibly strong arm. Schucker, even as he clawed at the limb that held him pinned to the table, marveled at the strength of the cult leader. He had never suspected the man to be so strong.

As Eon's fist crashed down again and again, Schucker's world began to fade to gray. "You…betrayed…me…." Dumar Eon said with each blow. "No one…betrays…Iron Thunder… with impunity."

"Please," Schucker managed to gasp. "Please…"

That brought Dumar Eon up short. "You…beg?"

"Please, Dumar," Schucker said, his vision doubled, his face swelling. Agony shot through every fiber of his being. He could feel something within him breaking, something very, very important. He felt a strange sense of disconnection from his pain-racked body.

"Very well," Eon said. "I want you to see this, anyway." He hauled Schucker up and turned him so that he faced the conference table. "Ladies and gentlemen of the board of the Security Consortium," he said, "I officially dismiss you. Your services are no longer required."

"Now, wait just a minute," one of the braver men said. "We're investors. You can't just cut us out."

"Can't I?" Dumar asked. He nodded, once.

The cultists attacked, using their knives.

"This is the best part," he whispered to Schucker. "Don't you think so? I regret I did not have this recorded. It would have made a fine Internet video. Don't you think? Well, don't you?"

When the screams finally subsided, Eon brought David Schucker's face close to his own. "Can you still hear me in there?" he asked.

"Please, Dumar…I—I…" Schucker stammered. Some portion of himself came back. "I…I was wrong. I only…

only wanted the company to grow. To make money. You like money, Dumar. Everybody likes money. I have some. I could...I could give it to you."

Eon ignored him. Still holding Schucker by the lapel in an iron grip, he gestured to the cultists. "Please, my brothers and sisters." He smiled. "Be seated."

Those board members who were still in their seats were thrown to the floor. The cultists sat down, ringing the table, looking back at Eon with all the worship they could muster. With bloody knives still clutched in their fists, they were a macabre parody of the men and women whose lives they had just taken.

"Wait a moment." He looked down at Schucker. "David, did you just try to bribe me?"

"Please, Dumar," Schucker wailed. "Please. Don't kill me. I don't want to die. Dumar."

"I cannot believe," Eon said with consternation, "that I could have been such a poor judge of character. David, David, David. I thought a lot of you, once, and even when I realized what you were trying to do, I could appreciate it. You at least had a certain dignity in your devotion to your purpose. Do you really mean to throw all that away now with this...this gross display? David, that is disgusting." He turned his attention back to his murderous followers.

"We have suffered much," the cult leader said. "I promised you a message. I can think of no better time to bring that message to the people. David here, probably believes that when his people stole my stockpiled chemical weapons, they got them all. What he failed to consider was that, given that I did not entirely trust him, given that I had reason to be suspicious for some time, I had some of those weapons moved. I had them cached in another location. And we, my brothers and sisters, can put our hands on those delightful tools of the gift of bliss. We can do so today. Does that not fill you with joy?"

The cultists voiced their eager assent.

"Are all of you committed, fully committed, to our cause? Understand that I am asking more of you than I have asked before. I am asking more than your willingness to take life. I am offering more than your own gifts of sweet oblivion. For today I intend to do something so remarkable, so indelible, that it will challenge the resolve of each and every person in this room. Are you still with me? Are you still my children?"

The cultists cheered.

"I'm glad," Eon said. "I'm so glad. Now, we are going to leave this place. As we do, I want you to set fires on every floor of this building. I want it burned to the ground, a testament to what happens to those who betray me." He paused. "Who here would like to tie up another loose end for me? There's someone I'd like to see removed from this earth. It's a matter of principle."

"Dumar…" Schucker spit blood as he tried to speak.

"Oh, yes," Eon said, looking perturbed. "I almost forgot about you, David. How rude of me." With Schucker pinned to the table, he struck the man over and over.

David Schucker's last sight on earth was Dumar Eon's leather glove as the fist inside it pounded the life from him. As the darkness closed in, he had just enough time to wonder if perhaps the Iron Thunder cultists had been on to something, after all, and to ask himself if he was truly prepared for the oblivion that approached.

And then he thought nothing more, ever.

16

"I told them you weren't hurt that badly," Bolan said from the doorway of Rieck's hospital room.

"You are all heart," Rieck said. He was sitting up in bed, watching television while going through some files that were spread on the blanket over his legs. He had a few stitches in his forehead. He wasn't wearing his shirt. His ribs had been taped up.

"Did a number on you, didn't they?"

"As you said it would, it got unpleasant." Rieck grinned. "But, Cooper, I have to say, working with you in the midst of this firestorm… I feel I've accomplished more genuine law-enforcement work in a couple of days than I have in the past two years."

Bolan had nothing to say to that. He looked out the window. Rieck's room had a good view of the parking lot below, and not much else. "They spared no expense, I see," he said.

"It's not bad," Rieck replied. "I wanted them to let me out last night, but they insisted on keeping me for observation. I had the office send over some of my files. I've been going through the old Iron Thunder data, cross-checking what we've learned since then."

"You should learn to relax when you can," Bolan said. "You never know when you'll get a chance to rest again."

"You sound like you speak from long experience."

"Been there."

There was a knock on the door. Bolan moved aside to allow an orderly to enter the room. He carried a bouquet of flowers in a small basket. With a nod, he left the flowers on the table in the room, where it joined two others.

"What's all that?" Bolan asked.

"Oh, that has been going on all morning," Rieck said. "The local papers have been reporting on the gun battles. As you might expect, it is one of the biggest stories this city has seen since, oh, I would say the Wall came down. It is not every night that war comes to the city so readily. Some of my friends within the police department were apparently too free with their accounts of the fighting, and my name came up. My superiors at Interpol, when reached for comment, have apparently seized on this opportunity for some positive public relations in the press. I am told I am to play the role of hero. I'm practically the star of my own spy novel, Cooper."

"So the flowers are…?" Bolan asked.

"From admirers." Rieck chuckled. "Gifts from a grateful public, thanking me for my service to country and to law and order. Apparently at least one news story explained that 'valiant investigator Agent Adam Rieck was recovering in hospital,'" he said sheepishly, "and there are only so many places I could be. They have been relentless this morning. There were calls for interviews, too, although the hospital switchboard is now preventing those from getting through."

Bolan frowned. He went to the table and looked at the bouquets closely.

"Cooper?" Rieck said. "Is something wrong?"

"No." Bolan shook his head. He looked up at another knock on the door; it was one of the doctors.

"Herr Rieck?" the physician asked. He was a younger fellow, Bolan noticed. His coat looked about a size too large on him.

"Yes, Doctor?" the Interpol agent said.

When the "doctor" put his hand in his coat, Bolan was already in motion.

"Eisen-Donner!" the man shouted. The Makarov pistol that came up in his hand swung on target.

Mack Bolan slapped it away, sending the weapon flying across the room. He followed with a brutal palm heel blow that knocked the assassin reeling, snapping the young man's head back and slamming him against the wall. The would-be killer shook that off and snapped open a switchblade. He crouched low, the knife moving back and forth in front of his body as he rounded on Bolan and took a step forward.

The soldier ripped the suppressed Beretta 93-R from his shoulder holster and snapped the safety off.

"Drop the knife," he said. "Get on your knees."

Rieck, looking on from his hospital bed, had the presence of mind to translate in German.

The assassin lunged.

Bolan put a single 9 mm round in his attacker's skull. He stepped aside as the corpse hit the waxed floor. Whipping his head around, he took in the doorway, which stood open and afforded a view of the corridor beyond. There were two more "doctors" approaching. When they saw him standing there, gun in hand, they reached into their white coats and revealed sawed-off shotguns.

"Down!" Bolan shouted. He slammed the door shut and dodged to one side. Behind him, Rieck threw himself off the hospital bed. He landed on the floor on the other side, groaning.

Shotgun blasts peppered the wall and shattered the window. Broken glass and fragments of plaster sprayed everywhere. Bolan, on the floor against the wall next to the door, waited for the first of the Iron Thunder cultists to come through the door. The man dived in low, thinking that would protect him. Bolan simply put a 3-round burst in the center of the crouching form.

The man slowly fell over, still crouched, and breathed his last. Bolan kicked the fallen shotgun across the floor, where it skittered under the bed in Rieck's general direction.

The Executioner considered his next move as another shotgun blast roared through the open door. The cultist who remained was standing outside, blasting away without aiming, afraid to enter but effectively keeping Bolan and Rieck pinned down. There were screams and shouts from the hallway and from neighboring rooms. Perhaps realizing that it was only a matter of time before hospital security and then police arrived, the cultist broke and ran.

"Rieck!" Bolan called. "Pick up that shotgun and watch the door for more. I'm going after him!"

"Right!" Rieck called.

Bolan was up then, jumping over the dead men on the floor and throwing himself out the doorway. He caught a glimpse of the fleeing cultist as he hit the fire door at the end of the hall. The metal barrier slammed shut.

Bolan raced down the corridor, stepped to one side of the door and opened it partway. A shotgun blast drew sparks from the metal face on the opposite side. Bolan waited and repeated the maneuver. This time there was no shot. He waited two more seconds, shut the door, then opened it yet again. Another shotgun blast tore paint from the door's surface.

The soldier ripped the door open. The gunner, on the landing below, was pumping the action of his shotgun, chambering the next round. Bolan put a 3-round burst into him. He managed to cry out before he collapsed.

There were more 12-gauge explosions from the direction of Rieck's room. Bolan ran back the way he'd come, holstering the Beretta and drawing the Desert Eagle.

A young man in street clothes and holding a snub-nosed revolver was using the side of the doorway as cover, trading shots with Rieck in the room beyond. Rieck triggered another shotgun blast. He had to be running out of ammunition. Bolan stood off a few paces and leveled the Desert Eagle.

"Hey," he said.

The Iron Thunder cultist turned in surprise. His eyes widened and his revolver came up. Bolan pulled the trigger, launching a .44-caliber slug that was the last thing the killer would ever experience.

"Rieck!" Bolan called.

"Yes?"

"Any more of them?"

"Not that I saw," the Interpol agent replied.

"All right," Bolan said. "I think we're clear." He took a moment to check the corridor. "Wait here a moment."

Hospital personnel were starting to emerge from the rooms on either side of the hallway, where they had taken cover and were trying to protect their patients. Bolan holstered his hand cannon and tried to be as reassuring as possible.

"It's all right," he said, "it's under control."

Bolan found Rieck still on the floor of his hospital room, the shotgun clutched in his hands.

"Still feeling accomplished?" Bolan asked.

"Jesus," he breathed. "What was that all about?"

"That," Bolan said, "if I had to guess, was Iron Thunder trying to make a point. I'd say they're upset you've repeatedly refused to die for them."

"Well, I do hate to be rude," Rieck wisecracked.

"Yeah, I've been accused of the same bad manners." Bolan bent to search the two dead men on the floor. He found nothing, except a spare magazine for the Makarov. The heavy Communist Bloc weapon was lying on the floor nearby. He cleared it and put the empty gun and the magazine on the nearby table with the flowers.

"Well, I won't say you never got me anything," Rieck said. He reached up and fished his phone from the pile of personal effects on the little nightstand next to his bed. "I'll start making calls. Again."

"Be glad you're alive to make them," Bolan offered.

"Well, it's clear to me I shouldn't be lying here when there are still people like that on the loose," he said. He stood and pointed to the closet. "Hand me my pants, will you? I am checking out."

Bolan found the man's slacks in the closet, as well as his shirt and coat, and passed them over.

Rieck grinned at him. "You know, Cooper, my local contacts have begun calling me 'Der Leichenbestatter.'"

"What does that mean?"

"The Undertaker."

It took some time to get things cleaned up, and Rieck was occupied for half an hour just making explanations and straightening things out with various cooperating law-enforcement agencies. When the bodies had been taken to the morgue and several more law-enforcement officials had crawled over the room with a fine-tooth comb, Bolan got a call on his secure phone.

"Cooper here," he said.

"Striker," Barbara Price said, "if you're near a television, you'd better turn it on."

There was a TV mounted to the wall in the corner of the room, where it could be seen easily from the bed. Bolan switched it on, Rieck watching him curiously. The picture was of a news anchor; the graphic on the screen behind her was the Iron Thunder logo.

Bolan switched channels several times, but news reports had broken in on almost all of the local channels. The soldier looked at Rieck.

"They're saying something about a major terrorist incident," Rieck said with concern. "And they keep mentioning

Iron Thunder. Wait, here it comes. They're saying the recording was posted on the Internet and was also sent directly to all media outlets in the city this morning."

The screen switched to a video of Dumar Eon. He sat in a darkened room, with the silhouetted logo of Iron Thunder behind him. His words, like those at the rally, were in English, but translated in German in glowing gothic script at the bottom of the screen.

"People of the world," the cult leader said, "I am Dumar Eon. Some of you know me. Some of you will deny me, but you, too, in your hearts, know. The great and terrible and wonderful responsibility of bringing to you the gift of my message, of bringing to you peace, of bringing to you nothing short of a new world order, falls heavily on my shoulders this morning. You will not understand, not all of you. But some of you will. Even as Iron Thunder, the organization I represent, shows you the way, builds you the way, burns you the way, cuts and stabs and shoots and chokes you the way, you may yet resist. But we are Iron Thunder, and we understand. We do what we do out of love for you."

Eon paused and held up a simple tourist postcard. "You see this place? This place is a symbol. It is a symbol of the old world order. It is a place where little people go to live their little lives, hoping to soothe the ache in their souls with possessions, with goods, with *things*. It is a place where those in need seek to medicate themselves until they are insensate, but never do those poor souls really address the true causes of their pain. It is for this reason that my people and I bring our message to those who are suffering this day. On this day, now and forever, those of you who persist, who go on after, will know that this is the day we began to bring you the beautiful gift, the blissful gift, the *only* gift. You will look to the ruins of what was and you will remember. You will long for that gift yourselves."

Eon held the postcard higher. The camera zoomed in on it. Bolan could see a glass-fronted building bearing the words Gropius Passagen. He looked at Rieck.

"That's a shopping mall," Rieck said. "Here in Berlin."

On the screen, the camera pulled back and Eon brought a gold cigarette lighter to the bottom of the card. He flicked it alight and began to burn the postcard. "On this day," he said, "the first of many acts of liberation begins. I am Dumar Eon. I am Iron Thunder. I am Iron Thunder. I am Iron Thunder... and so shall you be."

The video ended and the news anchor reappeared. The graphic behind her was replaced with a photo of the same shopping mall.

"This is confirmed?" Bolan said into his phone.

"Yes," Price said. "Iron Thunder took the Gropius Passagen mall this morning. The locals have cordoned off the area and are waiting for demands."

"There won't be any demands," Bolan said. "Eon doesn't want a ransom. He wants coverage. You heard him. He's got a wayward world that he wants to guide to the wonderful glories of being dead."

"We know," Price said. "Hal's burning up the phones trying to secure cooperation and advise the locals that they're dealing with a potential chemical weapons disaster, but they're not happy and they don't want to hear it. They're already on edge. You've been doing your best to burn the city down around their ears, the way they see it."

"Are they going in?"

"No," Price said flatly. "They don't want to risk losing hostages, like that schoolhouse in Chechnya. They'd rather try to cut a deal."

"We can't wait," Bolan said. "There won't be any deal, not with Dumar Eon. There's no telling what resources he could have brought to bear on this, but if the Consortium was selling nerve gas to the Syrians, Iron Thunder could have as much of it as they'll ever want or need."

"Understood," Price said. "We received all of your transmitted files. The materials at the Berlin safehouse were secured, of course. But you're right. There's no way to know what else could be waiting."

"I'm going to have to go in," Bolan said. "Tell Hal so he can try to clear a path for me. I'm putting an end to this right now."

"I know," Price said. "I won't tell you to be careful."

"Thanks," Bolan said. He cut the connection.

"Cooper?" Rieck said. "You're not actually going to… Oh, of course you are. Why do I delude myself?"

"It's been good working with you," Bolan said, offering his hand. "You're a good man, Rieck."

"You're not leaving me behind," the Interpol agent said. "I'm coming with you."

"It's going to get bloody," Bolan warned.

"What do you call this?" Rieck gestured to the room, which had suffered greatly under the pellets and bullets of the gun battle.

"All right," Bolan said. "Then let's go."

17

The Gropius Passagen, Berlin's largest shopping center, was a multilevel mall covering more than eighty-seven thousand square meters and boasting nearly two hundred shops and restaurants. Price transmitted a data file to Bolan's phone, with floor plans and whatever other useful data the Farm's computers had produced on the site. According to the data dump, the mall saw no less than sixty thousand visitors a day, on average. It was, in short, exactly the sort of high-profile target a terrorist madman like Dumar Eon would choose for a public massacre.

Rieck drove Bolan's rented BMW. He brought the car to a stop at the police roadblock, flashing his credentials to the submachine-gun-toting officers manning the cordon. He parked on the street, not far from an entrance to the structure.

The large, curved, glass-fronted entry was dotted with colorful signs proclaiming the names of some of the stores within. More police were stationed there. Rieck stopped and conferred with them; they were less suspicious than the first officers because the two newcomers had already been screened at the outer cordon. Finally, Rieck nodded to them both and then moved aside to confer with Bolan.

"All right, Cooper," Rieck said. He motioned the big man to a mall directory just outside the entrance. "I've got as much as we can get from them. We are here." He pointed. "They tell me Dumar Eon and his people have set up…here." He indicated another spot on the map. "That part is open. It's an atrium of sorts, where multiple levels are visible from the center. The Iron Thunder cultists have stationed themselves there—for what reason, we do not know. I am told we can get a view of this from the upper level. If we take these lifts—" he pointed again "—and then work our way over, we will be able to see them from relative concealment."

"Good work," Bolan said. "All right, let's move."

Bland music was playing over the seemingly deserted shopping center's speakers as the two men made their way to the elevators Rieck had identified. Price's data file had included the latest news updates available at the time, as well as some unconfirmed law-enforcement reports. Those tourists and other civilians who could evacuate already had. Eon had apparently taken quite a few people hostage, but his force was relatively small. He hadn't attempted to control the entire complex. The location wasn't well-suited to that sort of play, at any rate. It was too large, too open, with too many entrances and exits. No, the Gropius Mall would have appealed to Dumar Eon because it was a popular tourist attraction and, probably, because it was an icon of consumerism. It was the kind of public place that terrorists would be delighted to hit because seeing violence in such a locale upset people greatly. It was a blow to their sense of normalcy, a strike at the foundations of their routines.

Bolan didn't like the thought of being trapped in an elevator, but there was no choice. If they wished to remain undetected for as long as possible, they'd have to ride the elevator. The two men rode to the upper level in silence. The soldier checked his weapons and his spare magazines, shifting the war bag on his shoulder. He had been wearing his drover coat, but now he shed it. Rieck, likewise, dropped his trench coat. He had his MP-5 K on its shoulder sling, with several spare magazines in a pouch at his waist.

"You're getting pretty handy with that," Bolan said.

"I was always pretty good with the weapon," Rieck admitted. "I even participated in some practical shooting competitions with it. It's not the same. Even the targets that move. It's not the same at all."

"No," Bolan agreed. "It never is."

The chime of the elevator doors opening seemed loud to Bolan, but no one challenged their arrival. Bolan and Rieck crouched and made their way along the upper level, using the railing as cover. When they had gotten as close as they dared, the soldier peered into the atrium area. He could see the angles of the escalators converging as level topped level. The mall itself was impressive. Unfortunately, this relatively happy scene had turned into a horror, and Dumar Eon was the star of the show.

Bolan removed a small pair of binoculars from his war bag. With these, he carefully examine the tableau below.

The man behind Iron Thunder was standing on a stage, which, judging from the signs around it, had been erected for some sort of televised singing competition in the mall. He had appropriated the sound system for his own use and was speaking in rambling German. Feedback squealed. He had the volume all the way up and didn't seem to care. He paced the stage, gesticulating wildly, his long hair flying around his head like a lion's mane. He wore sunglasses and gloves, which looked out of place with his dark, tailored suit.

Strapped to his chest was what looked to be a bomb.

Specifically, it looked like the very same bomb the Iron Thunder cultists had affixed to Hans Becker, right down to the canvas rigging that held it in place.

A dozen other cultists circulated around the stage. They, too, wore bombs strapped to their chest. All were armed.

A few had shotguns, a few had assault rifles and many had submachine guns. Most of them were skinheads, and all were young males. Dumar Eon had apparently brought out the last of his shock troops for this mission. From their appearance, at least, they were hardened street toughs. Looks could be deceptive, but Eon wasn't playing around. He would have chosen his people for their ability to pull off the mission, and as Bolan and Rieck had seen, in most cases these were people who had no fear of death.

The hostages were at the foot of the stage. Bolan counted half a dozen of them. Each had a cylinder of some kind duct-taped to his or her chest. Duct tape had been used to bind the wrists and ankles of the prisoners, and to gag them as well. Some of them struggled weakly, but most knelt stock-still, as if any movement might make the canisters go off. There was no doubt in Bolan's mind that these were nerve gas units. If not nerve gas, it would be some other deadly chemical agent, something that would make a terrible and undeniable statement if it were released in the shopping center. There was no way to know how deadly the chemicals could be, or whether anyone outside the mall might be endangered. The only option was to make sure those canisters never disgorged their lethal contents.

Each of the canisters, Bolan could see through his binoculars, had a radio transmitter connected to it. He tracked the cult leader again. Dumar Eon carried what looked like the remote control to a DVD player in his left hand.

Eon began speaking in English, and he held a wireless phone to his ear. The soldier paused. The cult leader was talking to some media outlet, most likely, and every word out of his mouth reeked of falsehood.

"I guarantee the safety of your camera crew," he said. "Of course I do. There will be no need for violence, if only I can reach the right ears. For what is decisive action like mine geared to produce, if not results in the face of the powerful?

How am I, who am essentially powerless, to reach the media unless I do something bold? No, of course I will not harm any of your people. They will be guaranteed safe passage both into and out of the building. I will see to it. It may be necessary for me to threaten the lives of my hostages, but that is only to secure the cooperation of the authorities. No, no, of course I would not kill a hostage on television. Unless you think it would be good for your ratings? Hmm? You do not wish to say? Do not worry. Just come."

Bolan handed the binoculars to Rieck so the Interpol agent could assess the scene below for himself.

"Well," Rieck said finally, "that looks complicated."

"We have to do two things at once," Bolan said. "We have to stop them from detonating the bombs strapped to their chests, and we have to stop Dumar from using that remote."

"How do we do that?" Rieck asked. "I don't think we have time for you to disarm each one."

"Yeah, well," Bolan said, "it's easier when you're not trying to save the man attached."

Rieck considered that. "Then what you need is a distraction."

"Exactly right."

"Okay," Rieck said, "but if they beat me up again, I hold you responsible." He nodded and was gone.

Bolan turned back to the scene below and waited. Counting off the seconds, he figured the Interpol agent had had just enough time to work his way around again when Rieck appeared on the lower level. The cultists didn't notice him at first. When he spoke, his voice carried perfectly to where Bolan watched.

"Dumar Eon!" Rieck shouted, his voice surprisingly strong. "I have come because I believe in you!"

The cultists spun and brought their guns to bear. One of them might well have triggered a barrage had Eon himself not run forward, placing himself between Rieck and his people's weapons. The larger man stopped and looked down at Rieck, who held his hands out and away from his body.

"You come to me wearing a gun," Eon said.

"Yes," Rieck said, "but then, all of your people are armed. What does that matter?"

"Indeed," Eon admitted. "Tell me, little Interpol man, what do you want?"

"I've come because I believe in you," Rieck said again. Bolan was surprised; as he watched through the binoculars, he was tempted to believe the performance. Rieck had the look of devotion, the wide-eyed fascination, down perfectly. Bolan supposed the two of them had seen it more than often enough in the past couple of days.

"You believe in me?" Eon asked. "I find that difficult to accept."

"Why?" Rieck said. "You turned Ziegler. You've turned others. Is it so hard to comprehend that I would come to believe you, too? To accept your message? To desire the peace you offer?"

"If it is the peace of Iron Thunder you desire," Eon said, drawing a heavy revolver from inside his jacket, "let me give it to you."

"You don't wish to have a witness?" Rieck asked.

"What?" Eon said, confused.

"A witness," Rieck repeated. "There is no one here but your people and these hostages. You have no one to spread your message."

"That is unimportant," Eon said slickly. "The entire city, and soon the entire world, will know why we are doing what we are doing. I have seen to it. The message of Iron Thunder will be spread far and wide. And when I release the nerve gas into Berlin, the toxic cloud will kill thousands. Then I will destroy this place, and my people will know the final bliss. And forever after, our actions will stand as testimony to what we believe."

"Are you so sure?" Rieck asked. "Many great men have trusted history to write their epitaphs, and have been sorely disappointed with the outcome. Do you dare risk that?"

"So I am to believe you, suddenly, wish both peace and to ensure my legacy?" The revolver, which had drifted off target, snapped up again, pointed at Rieck's face. "Tell me, Interpol, where is your big American friend?"

"I killed him," Rieck lied.

"What?"

"I killed him, of course," Rieck said. "He was suffering. I wanted to bring him oblivion, as you preach. I did so. It felt wonderful. I want to know more before I join him and all the others. And I want to do justice to you."

"I don't believe you," Eon said.

"Well," Rieck said, "that's probably because I'm completely full of shit."

Eon cocked his head in confusion. In that split second of hesitation, Rieck sprang. He threw himself at the cult leader, grabbing the cylinder of the revolver with a death grip that kept it from turning, and stopped the gun from firing. At the same time, he snatched the remote control from the startled cult leader's hand.

They went down, wrestling for control of the weapon, while Eon clutched at the remote. The other cultists gathered around, unsure of what to do. They couldn't fire, for fear of hitting Eon. They were smart enough not to jump in or interfere otherwise, for the gun could go off in any direction. Paralyzed with indecision, they simply watched, fingers on triggers, waiting for an opening.

Above them, Mack Bolan drew the Desert Eagle.

The .44 Magnum pistol wasn't a sniper weapon, of course, but at this distance an expert and experienced marksman could hardly miss. The Executioner lined up the hand cannon's sights on the first of the cultists.

He fired.

The .44 Magnum slug screamed through the air. It struck the cultist in the back, punching completely through his body and destroying the bomb mechanism as it exited through the front. The perfectly aligned shot wasn't really an attempt to shoot the cultist at all, but to destroy the bomb he carried. The fact that the man was in the way of the bullet was only incidental.

The body hit the heavily waxed floor.

The cultists turned and opened fire.

They unleashed hell from their weapons. Bullets tore through the atrium. Glass shattered, metal sparked and lights were destroyed. Bolan calmly lined up the next shot with his pistol.

"Eisen-Donner!" they began to shout. *"Eisen-Donner! Eisen-Donner!"*

Bolan fired again, and a second cultist fell dead, the bomb on his chest a smoking ruin.

The cultists began pointing and shouting at one another in German. They started running for the escalators, intent on flanking Bolan or at least just reaching him. The soldier rolled, dodging a string of shots that ricocheted from the railing inches from his face. Then he was up and running for the nearest escalator.

He met the first of the oncoming cultists at the middle level, as the skinhead climbed the escalator two steps at a time to meet him. The man fired again and again, but his shots went wide. Bolan calmly closed the distance, targeted the cultist and put a .44 Magnum slug through his chest and the attached explosive unit. He kicked the body over the side of the escalator.

The other cultists rushed him, foolishly getting in one another's way as they funneled themselves into the killing chute of the rising escalator. Bolan leveled the heavy gas-operated pistol.

He triggered another round, and yet another member of Iron Thunder met his final reward with a broken explosive device strapped to his chest.

The gunfire began to converge on Bolan's location, but he couldn't let up. Tracking and firing, tracking again and firing again, he methodically worked his way through the cultists' ranks, aiming for the centers of the bombs and killing the men wearing them. The entire time, Dumar Eon struggled with Rieck on the floor below.

Bolan emptied the Desert Eagle. He reloaded on the move and continued firing. The noise was deafening as the shots echoed through the shopping center.

Suddenly, he realized the answering gunfire had stopped. The Iron Thunder members lay scattered and crumpled before him, their bombs deactivated, each of Bolan's shots having been as precise and deadly as the previous one.

He vaulted the escalator and used that to jump to the next, making his way to the ground level as fast as he could.

As Bolan raced to Rieck's rescue, Dumar Eon finally got the upper hand.

His body strength was greater, and once he managed to regain his balance, he found the leverage he needed, pinning Rieck beneath him. To do so he had to let go of the revolver. Rieck still had the gun by the cylinder, which did him no good; he would have to release it in order to change his grip. Rather than risk Eon getting it, he tossed it aside. Eon, however, was already grabbing for the MP-5 K strapped under Rieck's arm.

Rieck managed to fire a punch to Eon's jaw, but the cult leader barely noticed. He gave up on the subgun and simply wrapped both hands around Rieck's throat, ready to crush the smaller man's neck and end his life. Rieck, choking, threw the remote as far from them both as he could. Eon screamed in rage and tightened his grip.

Bolan walked up behind the cult leader and smashed the butt of the heavy Desert Eagle into his skull. Eon jerked and rolled off Rieck, dazed. Bolan planted a boot in his chest and stomped hard, knocking the breath from him.

"You okay?" he asked Rieck.

"Yes." The agent coughed, massaging his throat. "I will be. Did you get them all?"

Eon started to sob.

Bolan, careful to keep the man covered, holstered the Desert Eagle and drew the Beretta 93-R, which still had a full 20-round magazine. The fallen cult leader was holding his head and shaking.

No, Bolan realized. He's not sobbing. He's laughing.

"You fools!" Eon said, sitting up, on the verge of hysterics. "I've won, don't you see? I've *won!*" He looked across the atrium and spotted the remote control where Rieck had tossed it. *"Eisen-donner!"* he shouted.

The remote beeped.

Something on Eon's chest harness beeped.

The wireless detonators on the nerve gas canisters beeped.

The hostages screamed.

"Cooper!" Rieck shouted. "Voice recognition!"

Time compressed. For Mack Bolan, the entire universe slowed to a stop. His combat veteran's brain processed the variables involved and ticked down the numbers accordingly. There was only one thing he could do.

The Executioner fired a 3-round burst from the Beretta into the center of Eon's chest. Flicking the fire selector switch to single shot as he brought the gun around, Bolan, one of the most skilled snipers who had ever lived, put his reflexes and his abilities to the ultimate test. As if he could see the relays within the detonators closing, as if he could hear the imperceptible timing devices that were even now beginning their brief countdowns to release of the deadly chemicals, Mack Bolan lined up the first detonator in the Beretta's sights.

He fired.

And he fired.

He kept firing, snapping off single shots. The Parabellum rounds shattered each and every detonating device.

For Bolan, time started again. He drew in a breath.

The canisters sat there, inert. The stunned hostages looked at Bolan, their eyes fearful.

"Remind me," Rieck said, exhaling, "never, ever to make you angry, Cooper."

Bolan looked at him sharply. "Where's Eon?" he asked.

Rieck followed his gaze. Dumar Eon was nowhere to be seen.

The cult leader was gone.

18

Bolan ran after the cult leader. Rieck had remained with the hostages, to free them and to call in the authorities. Right now, he would be making sure the police knew that the hostage crisis had ended and that the ringleader was making a break for freedom. They would tighten their cordon and make sure Eon couldn't escape.

Bolan didn't intend to let the man get that far. There was a score to settle, and Dumar Eon had a lot of innocent blood on his hands. The Executioner was going to collect on that debt.

He caught sight of Eon ahead at the end of the wide, brightly colored hallway and quickened his pace. As he neared the spot where he'd last seen the other man, Bolan was rocked by a man-size projectile: Eon himself, who had doubled back, climbed a cell phone kiosk and thrown himself down from above. The two men rolled across the floor. Eon's sunglasses were crushed beneath them as they tumbled.

Eon ripped the canvas war bag from Bolan's shoulder and threw it away. He wasted no time wrapping his gloved hands around his adversary's neck. It was a strangely familiar sensation, but this man wasn't Bashir's bodyguard. That man had been heavy, tough and brutal, but he didn't have the animal

cruelty that flashed in Eon's dangerous eyes behind the snarled
locks of his long hair. Bolan looked into Eon's eyes and saw
the depth of the other man's evil.

"You will *die,*" Eon gritted. He was pale and sweating. The
rounds from the Beretta had smashed the bomb on his chest
and evidently failed to penetrate much farther, but they had
probably done him a considerable amount of injury nonetheless. He appeared to be in some kind of shock. Of course, it
was possible he was just in pain, and insane as well.

The man's physical strength was unbelievable. The tendons
in his arms stood out as he gripped Bolan's neck with viselike
power. The soldier's vision began to go dark around the edges
and he saw flashes of light.

He brought up the Beretta. Eon roared and trapped the
suppressor-equipped barrel with his neck, pinning the weapon
between his chin and his clavicle. Bolan pulled the trigger,
burning Eon's neck with the hot barrel, the rounds pounding
into a light fixture in the ceiling. Eon screamed from the pain
but kept the weapon trapped. As Bolan struggled to shift out
from under the cult leader, Eon wrapped his legs around the
Executioner's body, pinning him expertly.

"You cannot win, American," Eon gloated, his voice thick
through the pain. "I have spent hours building my body. I
have used the finest chemicals to augment my physique. I
have studied the fine points of grappling from experts in the
art. Jujitsu, wrestling, mixed martial arts… I am a weapon. I
will be the instrument of your death."

The Desert Eagle in its inside-the-waistband holster was
trapped beneath Bolan's body. The only movement left to him
was in his left arm, pinned to the elbow by Eon's hold. He had
only moments before he lost consciousness, but it would be
just enough. Drawing the Sting dagger from his waistband,
Bolan drove the knife up into Eon's right forearm.

The cult leader shrieked. Bolan drew the blade of the knife
up and around the other man's arm as Eon's grip slackened. A

blood-chilling scream escaped his lips. The cult leader rolled
away from Bolan, still screaming, holding his maimed arm
and swearing in German. Bolan looked down. The knife had
been torn from his grasp. Eon wrenched it from his arm and
threw it down.

"You fool," he managed to gasp. He clenched his own forearm in a death grip. Blood streamed through his fingers and
he was turning pale from its rapid loss. "Did you think I would
not have a backup plan? Where did you think I was running
to?"

Bolan looked around. There was an access door nearby, a
locked steel portal of the type used to hide mall access cor-
ridors used by staff. At Eon's words, the door opened. More
skinheads clad in bomber jackets and combat boots rushed
out. One of them handed Eon a backpack.

"Take him!" Eon roared. *"Kill him!"* He snarled in fury.
"I will not be thwarted, American! I will shout my triumph
to the skies!"

That, Bolan thought as he drew the Desert Eagle, didn't
sound good. He had lost the empty Beretta in the struggle; he
had only his knife and the rounds left in the big .44. Without
waiting, he put a Magnum round into the first of the skinheads, and then the second.

The Desert Eagle was empty and he had no more reloads.
His opponents squared off, undeterred by the sudden deaths
of their comrades. Eon limped off as the four men surrounded
Bolan moving in menacingly. One of them stepped over the
dead bodies of their fallen as if they had never existed.

One of the skinheads snapped open a switchblade. A
second had a pair of brass knuckles already on his fist. The
other two looked as if they would pull Bolan limb from limb
for the sheer joy of it. For whatever reason, Eon had held this
group back, perhaps knowing that if things went wrong, he
would need more muscle. Well, things had gone wrong, and he

was definitely benefiting from their efforts now. The soldier hoped that Eon would be stopped at the police cordon, but such things rarely worked out as they were supposed to.

Bolan prepared himself, balancing on the balls of his feet, with his knees slightly bent. The cultists were violent and they were tough, but they were amateurs. He could anticipate amateur mistakes.

The man with the knife lunged, trying to shove the blade into Bolan's abdomen. The soldier sidestepped the clumsy thrust, hooked the arm and slammed his right palm into the man's elbow. The joint snapped and the skinhead stumbled and fell, howling. Bolan had time to deliver a follow-up kick to the man's head as he tried to rise, putting him out of the fight completely. The knife fell to the floor.

Bolan dodged a brass-knuckled swing that would have taken his head off, only to take a knee to the stomach from one of the other men. He shrugged it off, hitting back fast and low with a series of brutal front kicks. The third man came in and went for the shoot, trying to tackle Bolan's knees and sweep his legs out from under him, but Bolan had been expecting that. He couldn't afford to let them take him to the ground and stomp him. Sidestepping the shoot, he balled his fist and punched the man as hard as he could in the junction between the skull and the neck. The skinhead sprawled on the floor and stopped moving.

One of the remaining two tried to scoop up the knife. Bolan met him with a kick to the face, then hammered an elbow down, bashing the skinhead to the floor with a sickening cracking of bone on bone. The man with the brass knuckles tried one last time. Bolan slammed his hands into the man's shoulder and inside his arm, stopping him short, and then hooked his right elbow through the man's face. The vicious blow sent him spinning. Bolan pursued.

The Executioner grabbed the stunned skinhead by the lapels of his bomber jacket, pulled him upright and slammed a palm heel into his chin. When the man dropped again, Bolan peeled the brass knuckles from his fist and tossed them aside.

The four men lay where they had fallen, unmoving.

Bolan took out his phone and dialed the number Rieck had given him. The Interpol agent answered on the second ring.

"Cooper?"

"Eon got away," Bolan said. "Can you contact the police outside and see if they've noticed anything?"

"I did already," Rieck said. "I've been talking to them since you took off after him. There's been no sign of him."

"Then he's in the mall somewhere," Bolan said. "And we have to find him. He's got something with him, and I have a sinking feeling his plan B is still explosive."

"The hostages are being debriefed by a special tactics team," Rieck said. "Where are you?"

Bolan rattled off the names of the nearest stores.

"I can find you," Rieck said. "There's a directory here. I'm on my way."

"No," Bolan said, "we'd better split up. Take the opposite end. We have to see if we can find him."

"Any ideas?"

Bolan thought about that. *To the skies.* Those had been Eon's words. "Look for roof access," he said.

He retrieved his war bag, reloaded his weapons, then found his knife. Cleaning the trusty Sting on one of the fallen skinheads' shirts, he sheathed the blade.

Satisfied that his opponents would be no trouble to anyone for a while, the Executioner continued on.

At the end of the corridor, he found a stairwell, which he took, leaping the stairs two and three at a time, moving upward. When he reached the stop, there were two doors. One led to the upper-most level of the mall. The other was marked

Dach. His German was limited, but he understood that much. The door moved readily, and he realized the lock mechanism had been pried open.

He pushed the door slowly.

Dumar Eon stood there, wearing the backpack on his broad shoulders. He was staring out over the city of Berlin. The gray of morning was giving way to a beautiful day as the clouds parted. Eon had lifted his face to the light and seemed to be soaking it in.

The Executioner raised his Desert Eagle.

"You won't need that," Eon said. He sounded strangely calm. From his position he could not see the gun, but it was a good guess.

"Turn around," Bolan said. "Slowly."

Eon did as instructed. His mangled arm was tucked into his suit jacket. He had wrapped a rag around it, but he was very pale and the rag was soaked through. He swayed unsteadily on his feet.

"Admit it," Dumar Eon said. "You are Phineas reincarnated."

Bolan said nothing. He had no idea what Dumar was talking about. "Lie down on the roof. Do it now."

"No," Eon said, smiling. He sounded strangely disconnected. Either the blood loss was taking its toll or he had ingested some drug. His face as almost beatific, as if he was experiencing supreme joy.

"Down!" Bolan said. "Or I will put you down!"

"Please do so," Eon said. "You see, I was wrong, American. I let my own pride come before the work. I never thought… Well, it does not matter now. But Phineas, he knew the way. When his work was done, he partook of the gift. It has been my time for too long now, but I denied that. Now I know it is my turn. Will you do this thing for me? Will you strike me down, so that I may know joy?"

Bolan didn't like the sound of that and he wasn't about to play this madman's games. "Eon, *lie down.*"

"I've told you no." Eon said. "What is so hard to understand about that? I intend to meet my gift with dignity. There were so many who did not. Even my...even my name. I am not Dumar Eon. I am Helmut Schribner. I should have been proud, but I was not. It was wrong."

He stumbled and then fell to his knees.

Bolan approached cautiously.

"What's in the backpack?" he said.

Eon looked up at him, ignoring the question. "Who are you, American?" he asked quietly. "What are you? How much death do you have on your hands? To how many have you brought the gift?"

"I'm not a charity," Bolan said. "I'm a janitor."

Dumar Eon laughed. "That is an interesting way to look at it." He coughed blood, the spasms shaking his body. "You have hurt me badly."

"I'll hurt you worse if you don't surrender."

"Oh, I have." Eon waved a hand. "There is nothing left. No more battle. No more cause. There is only the end. It is fitting that I meet the end with you. I have for so long believed death to be my companion, my tool, my reward. I see now that I was wrong. You, American. It is you."

"What?"

"You are *death,*" Eon said simply.

"Enough," Bolan said. The killing intent in his opponent's eyes was unmistakable. "The backpack."

"Another bomb, of course," Eon said. "It is counting down. The case is tamper proof. Any attempt to open it or to move it more than a few feet from my body will cause it to explode. The bomb has a sensor, keyed to my heartbeat."

"Shut it off."

"I cannot." Eon shrugged. "The timer, once started, cannot be terminated. I've given myself enough time to gather my thoughts. To enjoy my last moments. You may leave, if you do not wish bliss." He waved his hand again, weakly, a magnanimous king dismissing a subject.

Bolan considered that. Eon offered no resistance as Bolan searched him. He had no weapons, and his physical strength seemed to be ebbing moment to moment. Bolan risked leaving the cult leader where he was, running to first one corner of the roof, then another. An explosion up here might collapse a good portion of the mall. The hostages and some law-enforcement agents were still in the building. Bolan couldn't allow Eon to do any more damage.

At the third corner, he saw what he wanted. There was a marked police car below.

He took out his phone and called Rieck. "Rieck," he said when the Interpol agent answered. "I need you to square something with the locals for me. There's not much time." He explained what he wanted.

"They're not going to like it," Rieck said.

"Tell them about the bomb. Tell them what I'm doing."

"Will do," Rieck promised.

The agent called back a moment later. "You're good," he said. "Be careful."

Bolan closed his phone. He walked to Eon, grabbed him by the straps of his backpack and hauled him to his feet.

"What…what are you doing?"

Bolan dragged the cult leader to the edge of the roof.

And threw him over.

Eon screamed. He landed on the back of the police car, shattering the rear window and leaving a significant dent in the trunk. Bolan jumped after him, landing on the roof, bending his knees and rolling for the hood, every inch of his body jarred by the fall. His knee was wrenched, too, and would give him some pain, but he had survived. Eon was groaning weakly, lying in a dent the size and shape of his torso, covered in broken pieces of safety glass.

A German police officer had come running. He had keys in his hand, which he tossed to Bolan. The soldier caught them, climbed into the car and started it up. The abused cruiser responded despite the damage he'd dealt it. Bolan put his foot on the pedal and raced for the nearest point of the cordon.

The police units scrambled to get out of the way. Bolan slammed the pedal to the floor and brought the police cruiser screaming onto the street beyond the roadblocks, its siren hee-hawing and its LED lights blazing.

Dumar Eon groaned something unintelligible from the back of the car. He had made no attempt to move and probably couldn't.

Motorcycles came up on either side. Bolan looked left, then right. The men on the cycles wore helmets and leather jackets. He couldn't see their faces, but it was obvious who they were when the guns came out. Each man drew an automatic pistol from his jacket and started to shoot at Bolan. Eon made weak hand gestures at the pursuing cyclists. So the cult leader's backup plans hadn't included just the skinheads inside the mall; he had planned for an escort should he make his way to freedom.

Bolan wondered if these cultists knew their leader was a time bomb. If they did, would it make a difference? He wasn't sure. He didn't need to wonder how they had found him, though; in Eon's position, he would have stationed motorcycle teams near the major exits, and instructed them simply to pursue any likely vehicles or foot traffic that emerged. Bolan imagined that a half-crushed police cruiser with Dumar Eon planted in the trunk was a fairly obvious indicator that the cultists' services were desired by their leader.

The soldier squeezed as much speed as he could out of the damaged police car. There was traffic in the streets, and he was concerned about stray bullets and their danger to civilians, so he took a less-busy side street. There he parked the cruiser, got out and hid behind the engine block.

The motorcyclists rounded the corner, hot on his heels. He brought his Desert Eagle up, sighted, and fired, aiming for the front forks of the lead machine. The big .44 Magnum slug did its work. The front tire blew and the rear wheel drove the back of the light motorcycle up and over, throwing the driver onto the street, where the motorbike hit him for good measure. The second motorcyclist slammed into the overturned machine of the first, but managed to dump out without going down hard.

Bolan skirted the police cruiser, watching Dumar Eon out of his peripheral vision. There wasn't much time left, and he didn't want the bomb to go off on this side street, too close to the buildings facing either side. He dived left as the second cultist triggered several shots from his handgun. The answering .44 slug punched through the man's faceplate. He stood there, a marionette on cut strings, for a split second before dropping in a boneless heap. The helmet bounced on the pavement with a sickening thud.

Bolan grabbed the first man and dragged him to his feet. He put the barrel of the Desert Eagle under the man's chin.

"One chance," he said. "Give up."

"Eisen-Donner!" the man muttered. He bit down hard on something; Bolan pushed him away. The soldier had caught just the faintest whiff and knew that to breathe any more would be his death. Cyanide.

Shaking his head, he climbed back into the car. Eon was still groaning, but he had long ago stopped making sense. The soldier would have written him off completely, but suddenly he started speaking in whole words again.

"Wait! Pull…pull over," Eon said. "I was…wrong. I can…I can stop the bomb…. I… There is still time…."

There wasn't time, as Bolan saw it. Even if he thought trusting the cult leader was a good idea, the man was in no kind of physical shape to disengage the explosive he wore. His wounded arm had to be completely useless, for example. No, Eon had sealed his own fate. He could live—and die—with that knowledge.

The soldier scanned the streets as he drove. Finally, he found what he was looking for: a small, closed parking area, with no people in evidence and only a few vehicles. He slammed on the brakes. The car screeched to a halt on smoking tires. Then he shifted to Reverse, put the police cruiser as far from everything as he could, threw open the door and hit the pavement running.

"Wait!" Eon called after him again. "It is destiny! It is time! We must go to oblivion!"

"You first," Bolan said softly.

The police cruiser erupted in a fireball that broke out windows in every building on the block.

19

It felt good to be back in the United States. As often as he traveled abroad, Bolan always looked forward to coming back. This was the nation for which he had fought, and the nation for which he *still* fought. The battlegrounds had changed, the war had changed and the enemy constantly changed, but the reasons for his endless war never varied.

Bolan followed the coast road in his Chevy Malibu rental with the window down, enjoying the sunshine and the warm weather. A cool breeze relieved the heat of the day, and gulls wheeled above the Pacific Ocean. He had his secure phone pressed to one ear and was listening intently.

"We've had confirmations coming in for the last few weeks," Hal Brognola was saying. "The phones turned out to be the perfect tracking devices. International sweeps have been picking up Iron Thunder members in all of the industrialized nations. Even the Chinese had a few, it turns out, though they've refused our help and we'll never know into what hole they dropped the ones they found."

Bolan grimaced but let that go. "What about our friend in Interpol?"

"Who do you think has been coordinating the sweeps?" Brognola said. For the first time in a long time, he sounded almost cheerful. Bolan could picture the big Fed chewing an unlighted cigar, firmly planted behind his desk at his office in Wonderland. "A certain Adam Rieck sent a request through channels. He asked that, if anyone on this end could pass on a message to a Matthew Cooper, he wished to express his gratitude and to say he was, in fact, 'having fun.'"

Bolan chuckled at that. "Barb says the Germans gave him some kind of medal."

"They did," Brognola said. "It seems he's gotten most of the credit for the hits on Iron Thunder in Berlin."

"He *said* he'd take the heat for me."

"There's been plenty of that to go around," Brognola said. "Officially, the Germans are grateful for the intervention that has led to the removal of a dangerous group of terrorists. Unofficially, they're mad as hell. Between your war on them both and the fighting between the Consortium and Iron Thunder, there were so many bodies lying around that it looked like a zombie movie. The Germans are saying we unleashed a plague on them. Though they're not saying it too loudly to anyone but us."

"I'm sorry for your heartburn, Hal," Bolan said.

"Oh, I'll live," Brognola said. "I'm just glad it worked out as it did."

"What about the Consortium itself?" Bolan asked.

"Well, the government has been dickering about that for some time," Brognola told him. "It seems Dumar Eon—whose name really was Helmut Schribner, it turns out—was so thorough that there weren't any investors left to put in charge of the company. The government offered a buyout and there's been talk of partially nationalizing some of the Consortium's assets. At the very least, the strategic industries involved will be better protected from exploitation, from within or without."

"Well, that's good news," Bolan said. "And the Syrians?"

"Assan Bashir," Brognola said, "turned out to be the third son of the Bashir family, who are not unknown in the realm of international terrorism. They're reasonably wealthy, but more importantly, they've been maneuvering for years to try to stage a takeover of the Syrian government. A good old palace coup, if you will. I won't lie to you and say that State didn't consider whether the Bashirs could be used as an asset."

"I'm not surprised," Bolan said. "What came of it?"

"Nothing," Brognola said. "If anything, the Bashirs are even more hostile to the West than the current Syrian regime. And the rumors that they're sitting on those mysteriously disappearing Iraqi weapons of mass destruction would indicate that the Bashirs' possession of more such weapons didn't really deal the family into any high-stakes games. We eventually leaked information of the Bashirs' plans to the Syrians through indirect channels. I'm sure we can trust them to take whatever measures are necessary to remove the threat to their continuity of government."

"I'm sure," Bolan said.

"What about you?" Brognola asked.

"I'm almost there," he said. "How certain are we that this tip is legitimate? I don't see how it could be possible."

"We have several witnesses," Brognola said, "and the surveillance photos I'm looking at here would seem to back that up. I'm not sure how he managed it, but given where he is, it must have come at a serious price. The place isn't cheap, either, so he must have untapped resources."

"I'll see if I can get anything on that," Bolan offered. "It wouldn't hurt to have a few more dollars in the war chest."

"It's my job to worry about that," Brognola said.

"I know," said Bolan, "but every little bit helps." He cut the connection after a brief goodbye.

Bolan closed the phone. The GPS unit indicated that he wasn't far from his destination. It sat on a private stretch of California beach, which was in rare enough supply. Particularly beautiful stretches like this one were that much pricier.

Bolan hoped that his jeans, cotton shirt and light windbreaker wouldn't make him hopelessly underdressed. He didn't want to stand out too badly.

The services of the Ferrara Institute were among the best money could buy. The clientele of the small, exclusive facility was international, and had been rumored—according to Aaron Kurtzman's cyberteam—to include, from time to time, big names in the criminal underworld. Kurtzman reported that the clinic was currently treating only four patients, and three of them were women.

Bolan guided the Malibu up the drive and parked in the lot outside, between a foreign-made sports car and a silver Rolls-Royce. He examined the directory posted outside the clinic, then chose the left fork of a faux-stone path. The building was of Spanish design, complete with simulated stucco exterior.

Bolan checked in with the receptionist.

"Whom are you visiting, sir?" she asked.

Bolan flashed his Justice Department credentials. The woman looked unsurprised. "I don't know what name he might be using," Bolan said. He showed her a photograph.

"The man you want is in the garden," the receptionist said. "Through there, sir." She pointed.

"Thank you."

Bolan entered the large, enclosed garden, sliding the translucent glass doors closed behind him. A doctor and several nurses milled about. The three female patients were lying on lounge chairs in the sun, bandages wrapped around their faces. This was, after all, the nation's leading and most exclusive plastic surgery center.

Bolan surveyed the area and found the man he was looking for, lying in a wheeled lounge chair next to the pool. A chart was attached to a peg at the end of the chair. Bolan stood over the man and picked up the chart, reading through it.

"You're blocking my sun," the familiar voice said.

"Don't worry," Bolan replied. "We'll be leaving in a moment."

The single bloodshot eye visible beneath the bandages went wide. "You!" Dumar Eon gasped.

"Me," Bolan said. He looked down at the former cult leader. The man wouldn't be going anywhere under his own power; his chart indicated that he could barely move without assistance, and that every moment he tried would bring him exquisite agony. His face had been burned almost beyond recognition, and he had sustained considerable damage to the rest of his body. There was a litany of broken bones listed as medical history, relevant but unrelated to the various skin grafts and other repair procedures he had undergone or was scheduled to undergo.

"You didn't really think I'd just forget about you, did you?" Bolan asked.

"You *are* death," Eon whispered.

Bolan didn't answer. He found an orderly and made arrangements.

Twenty minutes later, a very uncomfortable Dumar Eon was strapped into the passenger seat of the Malibu. Under the disapproving glares of the orderlies, Bolan drove away. He headed back down the coast road.

"Where are we going?" Eon said through the haze of pain, as every bump in the road sent spasms through his body.

"You have a lot to answer for," Bolan said. "And I intend to see that you do. We're going to prison, Eon. It's no ordinary prison, either. It's the sort of place international terrorists go when we want to make sure they don't get out again. It's not someplace where your money will make one damned bit of difference. You won't be able to escape. You won't be able to bribe anyone. You won't ever see daylight again, Eon. You're going away, and you're going to stay there."

"That is not what you do."

"No," Bolan admitted. "But killing defenseless human beings is not something I do, either."

"Defenseless?" Eon said. *"Defenseless?"* His voice took on something of its former strength. "Do you think I was blown clear of that explosion, my body aflame, my mind screaming, my bones shattered, to be considered *defenseless* by one such as you?"

The former cult leader emanated raw fury; he was obviously of unsound mind, and that didn't surprise Bolan. "Do you think I allowed myself to lie in that gutter, dreaming of revenge, dreaming of the day when I would regain my strength and recommit myself to my mission, only to be dismissed?" Eon was screaming in his seat now. "I will have my day! I will bring my gifts to the world! I will not rot in your secret government jail! I will not go peacefully! I am Dumar Eon, and I will execute all humanity! I will execute them! I am an exterminator!" From within his bandages he snatched a front-opening switchblade. The blade came up fast.

Bolan was faster. He slammed on the brakes and whipped up the .44 Magnum Desert Eagle before Eon's knife could come into play.

A single shot to the head ended Eon's ravings.

"You may be an exterminator," Bolan said. "But I'm the Executioner."

JAMES AXLER

DEATHLANDS®

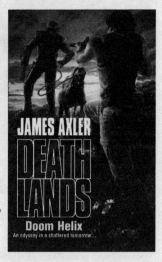

Doom Helix

A new battle for Deathlands has begun...

The Deathlands feudal system may be hell on earth but it must be protected from invaders from Shadow Earth, a parallel world stripped clean of its resources by the ruling conglomerate and its white coats. Ryan and his band had a near-fatal encounter with them once before and now these superhuman predators are back, ready to topple the hellscape's baronies one by one.

Available September wherever books are sold.

AleX Archer
THE DRAGON'S MARK

For everything light, there is something dark…

Archaeologist Annja Creed and her sword have never been outmatched—until now. An assassin known as the Dragon wields a bloodthirsty sword that should be feared. The Dragon initiates a terrible game of cat and mouse. Eventually the two swords, light and dark, must meet…and only one shall triumph.

Available September wherever books are sold.

GOLD EAGLE®

www.readgoldeagle.blogspot.com

GRA26